FOOLS IN LOVE

by

J. Sterling

FOOLS IN LOVE

Edited by:

Jovana Shirley

Unforeseen Editing

www.unforeseenediting.com

Cover Design by:

Michelle Preast

www.Michelle-Preast.com

www.facebook.com/IndieBookCovers

Please visit the author's website

www.j-sterling.com

to find out where additional versions may be purchased.

Thank you for purchasing this book.

I hope you enjoy my Fun for the Holidays collection!

Sign up for my newsletter to get emails about new releases, upcoming releases, and special price promotions:

Come join my private reader group on Facebook for giveaways:

PRIVATE READER GROUP

facebook.com/groups/ThePerfectGameChangerGroup

Other Books by J. Sterling

Bitter Rivals—an enemies-to-lovers romance

Dear Heart, I Hate You

In Dreams—a new adult college romance

Chance Encounters—a coming-of-age story

THE GAME SERIES

The Perfect Game—Book One

The Game Changer—Book Two

The Sweetest Game—Book Three

The Other Game (Dean Carter)—Book Four

THE PLAYBOY SERIAL

Avoiding the Playboy—Episode #1

Resisting the Playboy—Episode #2

Wanting the Playboy—Episode #3

THE CELEBRITY SERIES

Seeing Stars—Madison & Walker

Breaking Stars—Paige & Tatum

Losing Stars—Quinn & Ryson

THE FISHER BROTHERS SERIES

No Bad Days—a new adult, second-chance romance

Guy Hater—an emotional love story

Adios Pantalones—a single-mom romance

Happy Ending

THE BOYS OF BASEBALL

(THE NEXT GENERATION OF FULLTON STATE BASEBALL PLAYERS)

The Ninth Inning—Cole Anders

Behind the Plate—Chance Carter

Safe at First—Mac Davies

FUN FOR THE HOLIDAYS

(A COLLECTION OF STAND-ALONE NOVELS WITH HOLIDAY-BASED THEMES)

Kissing My Co-worker

Dumped for Valentine's

My Week with the Prince

Fools in Love

Spring's Second Chance

Don't Marry Him

Summer Lovin'

Flirting with Sunshine

Falling for the Boss

Tricked by My Ex

The Thanksgiving Hookup

Christmas with Saint

BEST AT MY JOB

APRIL

"ANOTHER SATISFIED CUSTOMER," I said out loud to no one in particular as I pressed on the keys of my laptop, closing out the file with the word *SUCCESS* stamped across it in bold red font.

My assistant, Meredith, walked by the moment I said the words, stopping abruptly in front of my office door. "Are you adding the client notes, or do you want me to do it?"

I looked up at her, smiling. "I got it. They're already done."

"You're a machine, April," she complimented me before walking away to handle her own set of tasks.

Her words made me laugh softly even though they were true. I was a freaking machine. And not only because

I was the best damn matchmaker in Manhattan, but also because I absolutely loved my job. There was nothing more satisfying to me than helping two people find love in this insane city. It seemed like it should be pretty simple with everyone always hustling and bustling around outdoors the way that we did here, but it wasn't.

Finding someone to screw was *easy*.

Finding someone to build a life with was *hard*.

There were other matchmakers in the city, of course, but no one had the record that we did. Our office was so good that we didn't even have to advertise. Everyone who came to us did so through word of mouth. I'd learned early on that when you did a good job for people and actually cared about the end result versus the money they paid you, it showed.

And it was valued.

My mentor and old boss, Sheila McHenry, had taught me that. She owned the company before I took over, training me in all of her ways while she groomed me, so to speak. And while she'd built up a reputation for being the best, I carried on the tradition, surpassing the old record of matched couples and new sign-ups.

Apparently, people were growing tired of online dating, claiming that all the same individuals were on every app. They wanted hands-on help, something different that proved to work and that was where I came in.

"April, don't forget we have that bachelor auction later." Meredith appeared in front of my office door, her ponytail swishing behind her shoulders as I blew out a long, annoyed breath.

I didn't do things like *bachelor auctions*. It wasn't my forte.

"Please tell me why we signed up to attend that again," I sincerely said because I couldn't for the life of me remember.

I would have never willingly agreed to attend something like that without good cause. I wasn't a fan of gimmicky type stuff. Especially when it came to things like single men being auctioned off for dates. It was supposed to be sexy and alluring, but I found it weird and off-putting. Even if it was usually for a charitable cause. It felt like it went against everything I stood for in my line of business.

I took dating and love a little too seriously to be able to enjoy an auction for what it was supposed to be—a fun night with a bunch of hot, available guys who were ready and willing … for what exactly, I wasn't sure. I'd heard rumors about what happened between the auctioned off and the buyer, but I had no idea what was actually true or not.

Meredith shook her head slowly, as if disappointed that I couldn't recall. "One"—she held up a single finger—"because of the charity they chose. They're helping all those missing people, remember? And two"—another finger—"because Sheila McHenry is the one putting it on."

Pressing my lips tightly together, I nodded in remembrance. It was a favor to the one person who had taught me everything I knew about matchmaking. The woman who had told me what was important and what wasn't when it came to finding lasting love for other people.

Sheila had told me that people often thought they knew what they wanted, but they didn't really have a clue. She said that most thought about love within four walls of a box, and it was our job to break down the walls and think outside of them.

When she sold me the company, she walked away, proud of what she'd built and hopeful for what I'd continue to do. But soon after leaving, she started hosting charity events. She'd quickly realized that being retired was supremely boring if she wasn't traveling twenty-four/seven.

"That makes sense. What time does it start, and what's the dress code?" Even though I didn't want to go, there was no way I'd ever tell Sheila no to something like this. I'd probably do whatever she asked me to until I took my last breath.

Meredith walked toward my desk, holding a lone sheet of paper. "I emailed you the details. They're in your calendar, already synced with your phone, but just in case, here's a hard copy."

It was considered old-fashioned of me, but I still liked to have some things printed out. It gave me comfort in a weird way to be able to hold information instead of studying a screen for it.

My eyes met hers. "You're coming too, right?"

"Yes." She smiled. "But unlike you, I'm flipping excited."

I grinned. "Of course you are."

Meredith was fun and funny, always up for a good time, and I imagined the idea of a slew of hot, single guys was right up her alley. Not that she'd have the funds to bid on anyone, but I figured she'd enjoy the atmosphere.

"You never know. Might meet Mr. Right tonight." She gave me a little dance before disappearing out the door.

"I highly doubt it," I whispered once she was gone, not wanting to burst her bubble, but it was unlikely that an event like this one could result in a real relationship.

That wasn't the point of it at all.

A one-night stand was more likely. And I wasn't interested in that either.

AUCTION NIGHT

ROBBIE

AS IF BEING a fireman wasn't exploitive enough, here I was, about to get auctioned off at a freaking charity event I had no interest in being at. I wanted to resist, but the fire chief would have my ass if he heard that I was being a little bitch about the whole thing. I had been told to suck it up, be a fucking gentleman to whoever was desperate enough to buy me for a night, and make sure they had a good time.

It was humiliating.

And don't get me wrong; I'd had plenty of action from the ladies over the years. Hell, I'd reveled in it not that long ago. Told any and every female I saw on the street how I was a fireman before asking if they wanted to slide down my pole. I know; I know, but most of them did want to slide down said pole.

You couldn't begin to imagine the level of attention we firemen got just because of our occupation. Women flocked to us in grocery stores, stopped by the firehouse with "treats," flashed us while we drove the truck, and stalked us on social media. They didn't know a damn thing about us, but none of that mattered.

We were *firemen*.

Hot. Dangerous. Men in uniform.

But one day, it'd all changed for me, and I could pinpoint the exact moment in time when my mindset had shifted. It was after the city calendar had come out, and I was unofficially named the Fire Hottie of the Year, as my picture graced not only one of the months, but the cover as well. If I'd thought women were easy to come by before the calendar released, it was nothing compared to after.

And I'd never been more miserable in my life than I was during that time. Every bit of attention was based on how I looked—how big my arms and shoulders were, how chiseled my jaw was, how ripped my abs were. The females of Manhattan didn't give a shit about my mind, my interests, my hobbies, or anything else. Hell, most of them didn't want to even have a conversation with me. All they wanted to do was be able to say they got to fuck the Fire Hottie and take a selfie or two to prove it to make their girlfriends jealous.

All of the meaningless sex had grown old. Pointless even. And it'd made me question my worth.

I know; I sound like a fucking female right now, but being exploited twenty-four hours a day, seven days a week, online and in person, eventually took a toll on your mental health.

Which was why I had absolutely no interest in perpetuating the shit show that was tonight's bachelor auction. Cap could have chosen anyone else in the firehouse. He knew how much I'd struggled post-calendar publicity, so I wasn't sure why he'd picked me out of all of the guys to do something as demeaning as this.

But again, I wasn't allowed to complain.

"Ready for tonight, Mitchell?" my captain asked with a hard slap to the back.

I suddenly wondered if he was going to be in attendance to witness my humiliation in person. Why hadn't I thought about that before?

I tried not to choke on the thought of him being in the audience. “Sure.”

“Don’t sound too excited.” He frowned.

“Oh, I am, sir. Incredibly excited to take some strange woman out for what I’m sure will be an overly romantic evening, where she’ll care about what I think instead of how I look,” I answered, sarcasm dripping from every syllable.

“Damn, Mitch,” he said, shortening my last name for emphasis. “You don’t have to be so cynical.”

“Cap”—I reared my head back and gave him a look—“I’m going to be bought tonight. Purchased. Like cattle. Like I’m nothing more than a piece of meat to go on someone’s dinner table.”

“There are worse ways to spend a Tuesday night. Stop being a sissy and start being thankful,” he said, his tone forceful, before he walked away.

Thankful?!

Thankful for what? I thought to myself.

I wanted no part in this.

“Hey, Cap,” I shouted, and he stopped walking, so I knew he was listening. “How’d we get sucked into this anyway?"

I'd been here almost nine years, and we'd never participated in this kind of thing before. No one else in the firehouse had been auctioned off for charity in the past, so why were we suddenly doing it now?

He turned around, his dark eyes meeting mine. "It's a favor for a dear friend. You will be on your best behavior and do whatever you're told. And I do mean, whatever. Besides, she requested you specifically."

"Why would she do that?" I asked, wondering if it was the curse of the calendar continuing to haunt me.

"The hell if I know," he said before heading upstairs.

This was going to be the worst night ever.

HERE GOES NOTHING

APRIL

I HAD NO idea what to expect, but the event space I walked into wasn't it. It was gorgeous—dare I say, classy even. Floral arrangements filled the room, candles were glowing, and twinkling lights dotted not only the trees that had been brought in to mimic a miniature Central Park, but they were also spread throughout all of the decor—from the multiple bars to each entryway and exit.

There was a large stage, obviously, for the guys to eventually strut their stuff all over, and seating was set up all around for what I assumed would be a plethora of screaming women.

Do women scream at this kind of thing?

The chairs were pretty though with white tulle and overstuffed padding. It looked more like a high-profile wedding reception than what would be a bachelor auction. I wanted to smack myself silly. Of course this wouldn't be some rinky-dink affair. My old boss was in charge of the event.

Speaking of, I noticed Sheila in the distance, laughing with some ladies as she sipped what looked like a glass of white wine. Her head tilted up, and I knew the second she spotted me.

I watched as she excused herself and started speed-walking in my direction as fast as her high heels would allow.

"April, darling." She gave me a kiss on the cheek. "You look gorgeous. What do you think?" she asked, waving a hand around the room.

"You've outdone yourself," I complimented, knowing how much she thrived on words of affirmation. It was her love language. "It's not at all what I expected."

Her bright blue eyes scanned my face before a grin lit up her face. "And what did you expect? Some trashy number? You know me better than that."

She mocked offense with her questions, but I only shook my head before responding, "I've never been to something like this before, so I was picturing more *Magic Mike* and less JFK Jr. wedding reception."

Her smile suddenly dropped. "I always liked that boy. Tragic, losing him that way. And those poor girls."

My mind instantly flashed back to all those years ago—when the city of Manhattan had mourned the loss of their golden prince. His death had cast a long shadow over the city that lasted for weeks.

"I see you have your number." She changed the subject, tapping the auction paddle I held at my side.

I'd been given it upon check-in, even when I'd said it wasn't necessary and that I didn't need it. Apparently, everyone in attendance received one regardless of whether or not you intended to bid on a stranger.

We had also been given a brochure, detailing each bachelor's name, occupation, and where you got to go on your date if you were the winning bidder. I'd had no idea how planned out these things were. I'd just assumed that if you won the guy, you figured it out on the fly and did whatever you both wanted.

Not in this day and age. No detail was left to chance. Every single aspect was meticulously prepared. Safety was the number one priority. It even said so on top of the brochure.

"I really don't need it." I waved the paddle in my hand, but she smiled a little too smugly, and I wondered what she was up to.

"Trust me, April, you do."

I had no idea what that meant, but she turned on her heel and told me she'd see me before the auction started.

What the hell was I supposed to do until then?

I DON'T WANT HIM

APRIL

WHEN MEREDITH FINALLY arrived—dressed to the nines, I might add—I let out a sigh of relief. No longer was I standing in the corner alone, avoiding all contact with people I didn't know, checking my emails incessantly, pretending like my work couldn't wait a few hours.

"Your hair looks so pretty," she complimented the waves I'd spent hours putting into my long hair, and I instantly ran my fingers through it.

"Thank you. Your dress is beautiful." I eyed her from head to toe, giving her a grin and an approving nod.

"Thanks!" Meredith said with a smile of her own. She held her numbered paddle in the air. "I love this thing. I can spank whoever I buy with it."

A thick laugh tore from my throat. "Oh my God. You're insane."

"But in a fun way." She waggled her eyebrows and waved her paddle through the empty air.

"You're not going to really bid on someone, are you?" I asked, never considering the option before this moment.

She shrugged. "Maybe? It depends," she added before looking around. "All the women here look rich. Like, really rich. I'm not sure how much my hundie will get me." She pulled a hundred-dollar bill out of her bra and flashed it in front of my face.

I realized that Meredith was right though when I finally scanned the crowd. I recognized multiple women CEOs and other high-profile philanthropists. "I think you're right. That might get you a shoelace. Or a hat."

Meredith huffed out in disappointment. "Maybe they'll have one guy for the poor girls in the room?" She actually sounded hopeful even though I was sure that wasn't how this sort of thing worked.

"Guess we're about to find out," I said as Sheila stepped onstage and started tapping a live microphone, the sound echoing throughout the space as everyone immediately quieted down.

"If everyone could grab a seat, we'd like to get started soon," Sheila said, and a few women hooted in the background, which made her smile. "I'm glad you're excited. I'm excited too. Just keep in mind that all of your winning bids and donations in the silent auction are going to benefit The Missing. I want to personally thank each one of you for coming. Thank you to the bachelors, who have donated their time. And to all the sponsors, who so graciously contributed the winning dates and transportation with very little arm-twisting from me. Make sure you visit them. They're all listed in the back of your brochure."

"Come on." Meredith grabbed my hand and pulled me toward some empty seats near the front of the stage.

Even though I was mortified to be sitting so close, I followed her without complaint and sat down.

Sheila appeared out of nowhere, asked the woman next to me to slide down one seat, and sat.

"You're sitting with me?" I asked.

"Meredith makes me laugh. She'll be entertaining," Sheila said, as if she were intimately aware of Meredith's personality.

I stared back at the stage, which was way too close for my comfort.

"Plus, I enjoy watching you squirm, April."

I whipped my head to the side and gave her a narrowed look. "I don't squirm," I argued defensively.

Sheila gave a soft nod. "You most certainly do whenever you're uncomfortable, which isn't often, but you have been since you walked through the door tonight. Hovering in the corner like I put you in a time-out."

I fought off the words to disagree with her and choked them down instead. There was no point. She was right, and we both knew it.

The house lights went out without warning, and only the candles and mini twinkling lights remained. Music started, loud and overbearing before lowering as an incredibly well-dressed man stepped onto the stage and into the single spotlight that flicked on with a hum.

"Ladies and …" He paused, placing his hand over his eyes to block out the light and look into the crowd. "Well, ladies and ladies," he said with a loud laugh, and I realized that there were no other men here.

I wondered if Sheila had planned it that way before realizing that, of course, she had. She controlled every aspect of anything that had her name on it.

"Couldn't have the men competing with us here too. Tonight is about making the male gender subservient to ours. We're the bosses. They do what we say. They belong to us. And it's about damn time," Sheila said.

She sounded so proud, and I shifted in my seat, more than a little uncomfortable with the gender war. Not because it wasn't true and there wasn't one waging, even silently, but because I didn't participate in it. If anyone tried to hold me back, I bowled them over—man or woman, it didn't matter to me. The only war I played in was the one against myself.

The music continued in the background as the emcee introduced the first bachelor of the evening. He was dressed in a tuxedo, looking mighty dapper, and I swore the audience swooned at the sight of him. He hammed it up for the crowd, dancing and doing little spins. I stopped myself from rolling my eyes, but only because I could feel Sheila's gaze on me.

Bored, I opened the brochure to read the guy's name.

Austin Steel. Apparently, he was one of New York's finest. A police officer.

"Are all these guys single?" I whispered toward Sheila.

"Don't try to scout them for the agency, but yes. I can see the wheels spinning in your head. Stop them."

I'd honestly just been curious, but now that she had mentioned it, getting all these guys signed to the agency would be good for business. If they were looking to have actual relationships instead of just hooking up, I could market the hell out of that. I could create an entire Men in Uniform category of the matchmaking business.

"April," Sheila practically growled in warning.

I held up a hand. "I'm stopping. Promise."

The auction was proving to actually be entertaining. Women got into bidding wars, screaming at one another as they fought over who could raise their paddle the quickest. Meredith kept hers firmly in her lap, the price growing way too steep, too fast. She had been right about her hundred-dollar bill getting her nowhere. At least in this crowd.

Before I knew it, the last bachelor was being announced.

"Ladies, this is the last bachelor of the evening. I hope you're ready for him," the emcee teased, playfully toying with the already-riled-up women.

I breathed out a quick sigh of relief that I'd managed to make it through the evening unscathed when the air suddenly caught in my throat at the sight of the guy now standing onstage. It wasn't that he was good-looking because every single man on that stage tonight had been conventionally hot. Each one could have been on a magazine cover, but that was Manhattan for you. Gorgeous men lurked around every corner.

The chiseled, dark-haired guy up there now looked uncomfortable.

Agitated.

Angry even.

And for whatever reason, his ire drew my attention right to him.

He didn't want to be here. At least we had one thing in common.

"That's Robbie Mitchell. He's a firefighter." Sheila leaned toward me, and I nodded because the emcee had just informed the room of the same thing.

"I heard."

"He works with Captain Alvarez," she said, and all the pieces suddenly clicked together as the emcee started the bidding.

Sheila and Captain Alvarez had some sort of romantic history between them that neither one ever spoke of, but anyone with eyes could see it. Whenever they were in a room together, you could almost hear the air crackling with sparks.

"Why didn't you ask him to be the bachelor instead of one of his younger guys?" I asked, knowing that the question would irritate her to no end.

She shot me a look that would have killed weaker people on the spot. "You know why," she responded.

Before I could even savor in my win, Sheila was reaching for my arm and thrusting it into the air.

"Five hundred fifty dollars to number one-two-three," the emcee shouted before pointing at another woman across the row from me, who was upping the ante.

"What the hell?" I yanked my arm out of Sheila's grip, but she did it again without warning, and the announcer focused his attention back on me. "Stop making me bid!"

I made the mistake of looking toward the elderly woman on the other side of the room, who I was suddenly in battle with. She glared at me, pointing two of her fingers from her eyes to mine, and I turned toward Sheila, wondering what the hell she'd gotten me into and why.

"That old lady over there is plotting my death."

"She'll get over it," she said before forcing my arm up again.

How the hell is she so strong?

"She's going to poison my drink," I whisper-shouted as I dropped the paddle, not wanting to die at the hand of some bitter grandma who had nothing left to lose.

I realized too late that letting it go was a stupid move instead of a smart one. Sheila picked it up and kept on bidding until my number was declared the winning bidder—at over three thousand dollars! I sure as heck wasn't paying three grand to go on a date with Mr. Sourpuss up there.

Right when I was about to let Sheila know exactly that, she stood up from her seat and said, "I'm going to go write a check for your bachelor. I'll be back to introduce you."

"I don't want him! You keep him! It was your bid!" I

shouted at her, but she waved me off and continued walking away.

Meredith couldn't stop laughing. Her arm was wrapped around her stomach as she bent in half.

"I will fire you," I threatened, and that only made her amusement grow.

"No, you won't. Oh my God, April. That was the funniest thing I've ever seen. Your face." She kept trying to talk, but she could barely get the words out through her fits of giggles.

Speaking of faces, I moved my gaze toward the stage just in time to see Robbie, Mr. Sourpuss Firefighter, glaring at me with narrowed eyes. He didn't look the least bit happy or entertained.

You and me both, buddy.

GREAT, JUST GREAT

ROBBIE

WHAT AN ABSOLUTE *fiasco.* As if standing on a stage, being auctioned off, hadn't been humiliating enough, there ended up being a "war" to win the date with me. I'd garnered the highest bachelor bid of the night, which earned me some sort of unspoken honor. I should have been flattered, but trust me, I wasn't. Even if it was for a good cause.

Watching the elderly woman and the hot brunette go at it for a piece of me really should have gotten me at least a *little* hard, but per usual, it'd made me feel cheap and sleazy. I had no idea why the gorgeous girl near the front of the stage would need to bid on anyone for a date in the first place. Her long, dark hair spilled across her bare shoulders, and I imagined briefly what it might be like to wrap my fingers in it as she sucked me off.

The determined look on her face each time she threw her paddle in the air was fascinating. She looked angry. Like she might kill the older lady if she outbid her and won the date with me. The oddest part was that her expression never shifted. Not even after she placed the winning bid. I had no idea what it'd all meant, and I really didn't want to find out, but I guessed there was no choice now.

I belonged to her.

For a night to be determined in the near future, or something to that affect.

"Ms. McHenry would like you all to mingle with the donors now," the emcee of the event informed all of us guys who were happily hanging out backstage.

Or maybe I was the only happy one to be behind the scenes, out of view, because no one groaned or complained or even let out an annoyed sigh at the request. All the other men seemed content to be doing this. I was apparently the only one with an issue.

An NYPD officer walked up to me and slapped his hand on my back in some sort of congratulations. "I think you got the hottest woman in the room. At least your date will be fun. Did you see who won me?" he asked with a laugh.

I shook my head because I hadn't paid attention to anyone else. "Sorry, man, I didn't catch it."

"She's a bit out of my age range, but she's probably nice, right?"

I wasn't sure if he was sincerely asking or not, so I didn't give him a response.

"Not sure she's going to be able to bowl though."

"Bowl?"

"Yeah. My date is dinner and bowling. What'd you get?"

Running my hand across my eyes, I hesitated before telling him. I knew he'd be jealous. I'd read the brochure front to back while I waited for my turn onstage. Out of all of the dates, mine was hands down the best one, in my opinion.

"You're gonna be pissed," I said, and his mouth formed a frown.

"Tell me," he insisted.

"Dinner at Tavern. Private skating at Wollman. Serendipity for dessert," I recited what I'd read in the pamphlet as nonchalantly as I could muster, but his jaw clenched shut anyway. I couldn't have missed his reaction if I'd tried.

Tavern on the Green was a New York staple. A historic landmark in the heart of Central Park that was seeped in history and luxurious dining. Most people didn't go there on a first date unless you were planning to propose after. And Serendipity was just as famous, known for its frozen hot chocolate and that stupid movie people couldn't seem to get enough of.

"Not fair, man."

"I know. I told you."

"Time to mingle," he said before giving me a head nod and heading out one of the doors.

I contemplated staying here, wondering if anyone would notice my absence at all. But before I could make a decision, Sheila McHenry appeared backstage, her eyes searching for someone before landing right on me.

"Ah, just the bachelor I was looking for," she said, and I forced a smile.

"And why's that?"

"I want you to meet your date." She grabbed my arm, wrapping hers through it as she led me out of my safe space and into the crowd.

WHAT AM I SUPPOSED TO DO WITH HIM?

APRIL

I SPOTTED SHEILA closing in on where I stood with Meredith, a vodka tonic in one hand, which I quickly finished off before she reached me. She was arm in arm with none other than the guy *I'd* apparently bought a date with. He was freaking gorgeous, and I lost myself for a second, thinking about how fucking hot he must look in his firefighter uniform.

The man was a work of art. And I suspected that he knew it.

"April, this is Robbie. Robbie, this is my brilliant protégé, April. I'm sure you two have a lot to talk about and coordinate," Sheila said, and I sensed that she was about to walk away and leave me alone with this guy who looked like he wanted nothing to do with me.

Reaching out, I grabbed her arm before clearing my throat. “Technically, he’s your date since you paid and all. Right?” I focused my gaze on Robbie before adding, “I think she wanted to go out with you, but didn’t want anyone to know, so she used my paddle instead of her own. That way, no one could gossip about the young stud Sheila McHenry bid on at her own event.”

I was talking a mile a minute, and I had no idea why.

Does this guy make me nervous? And if so, why?

“Isn’t that right?” I asked, my voice cracking as I met Sheila’s amused grin.

“No. That’s not right. He’s a gift. For you. You’re a gift. For him. You’re both here for each other.”

My face had to look as confused as I felt. Sheila reached for Meredith and said something I couldn’t hear, and they left before I could ask her any more questions. I’d grill Meredith for information at the office tomorrow. She was *my* assistant after all.

“That was weird. Is she always that weird?” Robbie asked.

I shook my head. “No. Never.”

Sucking in a breath, I took a long, hard look at the man who was supposed to be my gift. He towered over me, which Sheila knew was my first downfall in a man. I loved a tall guy. His dark hair was cut short, and he had a beard to match. That facial hair was a work of art, perfectly aligned along his jawline, making it appear even sexier somehow. He had green eyes. Another thing known to ruin my decision-making skills. What was it about green eyes on a man that made women turn to dough?

His body looked like it had been made by an Italian carver. If they erected a statue out of his physique, millions around the world would worship at its feet. Not me, of course. I'd admire it from afar. Maybe take a picture or two.

The sound of fingers snapping drew my attention, and my cheeks felt a hundred times hotter in that instant.

"Sorry, I was distracted."

"I noticed," he said, his lips not even remotely turning up to smile. He was irritated.

"I wasn't …" I stumbled on an excuse to give him that I knew he wouldn't buy. "Never mind."

He leaned toward me. "I could look at you the same

way you just looked at me. Like you're nothing but a hot piece of ass with a set of great tits. I could jack off for days to the image of those perfect lips wrapped around my cock, sucking me off." His words hit my ear in a way that caused the hairs on my arms to stand on end with warning.

I pulled my head away from his lips, my mouth suddenly dry, my stomach on the floor. It had been a long time since anyone had been so vulgar toward me. At least, not without my wanting it.

"Does that make you feel good about yourself? To know that I see you as nothing but a shell I'd love to fuck, make come, and never talk to again?"

"Jesus. Stop it," I complained, and that earned me the tiniest smirk.

"Ah, so you don't like it." He sounded smug. Proud of himself.

Shifting my weight from foot to foot, I met his judgmental gaze. "I don't like it. I don't even know you."

"Welcome to my world." He blew out a breath.

"I take it, you don't want to be here."

He looked around at the room, the frown back on his face. "Great observation, Captain Obvious."

This guy was an absolute prick.

Nice gift, Sheila. You can have it back. I sure as hell don't want it.

"For the record, I didn't want to come tonight either. This isn't my scene or something I'd normally attend. I did it as a favor."

A strangled laugh escaped from somewhere deep in his throat, and I watched as his Adam's apple bobbed. "I can see that. Winning bidder of bachelor number seventeen."

"I already told you"—I started to get fired up—"that wasn't me."

He stood tall and sucked in a breath before pinning me with those green eyes. "Then, how come I don't believe you?"

"I couldn't care less what you believe."

I looked around the room and noticed the older woman I'd been in the bidding war with staring at us. The second I caught her watching, she put her drink down on the table and fixed her dress with her hands before heading our way.

"Looks like your admirer is coming to claim her prize. I'll happily give her the date, so you can take her out instead."

Robbie suddenly looked like a deer caught in headlights. His eyes grew wide as she closed in on us, and I swore he checked all the exits for the nearest escape, but it was too late.

"Don't you fucking dare," he ground out through clenched teeth just as she reached us, her body like superglue to his side as she wrapped her arms around his biceps and squeezed.

Robbie honestly looked like he might be sick.

Oh, this was going to be fun to watch.

THE HELL IS MY PROBLEM?

ROBBIE

I WAS PUNISHING April for … well, I was punishing her for existing. When I had seen her eyeing me from head to toe, I'd gotten triggered. She was just like every other female, all caught up in my exterior and giving little to no thought about anything else.

I told you already, I was a little fucked up.

Now, I was being pawed by the elderly woman who refused to stop touching me wherever her fingers decided to explore, and I had to just stand there and take it. April couldn't stop smiling. She was enjoying this. My discomfort and unease.

"It's a pity I lost," Grandma Darcy said before squeezing my ass so hard that I figured it would bruise.

Okay, so her name wasn't really Grandma—I'd added

that part—but it was Darcy. It said so right on the name tag pinned to her right breast. Which was threatening to topple out of her dress at any moment. The left boob was firmly in place behind the tight fabric, but the right one was spilling out of the top all haphazardly, demanding to be free.

Please don't.

"I'm sorry you lost too," I lied, giving April a quick glance that warned her not to say a word.

If she gave Darcy our date, I'd hunt her down and make her pay. *Somehow.* Revenge wasn't my strong suit, but I was sure I could learn a few tips online, maybe read some books on the subject.

"It really came down to the wire, didn't it?" She was talking to April now, her tone turning more than a little passive-aggressive. "I feel like we could have gone back and forth all night long. I bowed out gracefully because I already know where to find him after your date is all said and done."

Grandma Darcy licked her lips, and I pictured it in my head without any effort—her showing up at the firehouse, that right boob swinging free for all to see, her telling me all the things she wanted to do to me, my fire captain making me oblige her requests.

"Yeah. You can't blame me for not wanting to let this one go," April said sweetly, adding a wink at the end before she placed her hand on Grandma Darcy's shoulder. "Thank you so much for *letting* me win."

The subtle dig was not lost on me.

"I figured you needed it more than I did."

Damn. Women never stop being mean to each other, do they?

"You got that right. All I do is work. No time for a social life. This will be a great distraction. If only for one night. It's just what I need," April continued to explain, and I wondered just how much of what she was saying was true and what was being fabricated.

I focused on her, taking in everything about her. She did seem like the workaholic type, sort of uptight and serious.

"I guess I'll let you two get back to whatever you were doing before I came over and added some necessary spice to the mix," Grandma Darcy said.

Before I could even respond, her lips were on mine,

moving back and forth like she was trying to wipe off all of her lipstick onto my mouth. I swore that if her tongue made an appearance, I'd scream like a little girl, high-pitched and everything.

I stood there, unmoving, my eyes wide open and firmly locked on to April's face, which was a mixture of shock and horror. Before I could give her a look that screamed for her to do something, Darcy stopped assaulting me and promptly left.

April moved in immediately, closing the space between us as her eyes widened. She stared at my jaw, her hand lifting to run across it before she instantly dropped it back to her side. "Your face is a very pretty shade of rose."

"There's lipstick everywhere, isn't there?" I managed to ask through my complete embarrassment. "Help me."

I refused to look away from her hazel irises to see if anyone else in the room had witnessed my humiliation firsthand. I wouldn't be able to handle it, to be honest, so I kept staring. Her eyes became my lifeline, the only thing I saw in the room. She had flecks of green and yellow in one eye only, and I wondered for a minute if she knew. I thought about telling her.

"It's all over your face. Literally." She reached for my arm and started pulling at my body, trying to get me to move. "Come on. Let's find a restroom."

My legs started moving of their own accord, clearly willing to follow this woman anywhere she asked. Ten minutes ago, I would have complained, fired back some sort of sarcastic comment, but I needed her help now. We weaved through people, not stopping for anything or anyone as I focused on my steps.

Next thing I knew, we were stopped in front of a large, nondescript wooden door. April reached for the handle and pulled it open before peeking inside.

"It's empty," she said as she held it open for me.

I walked through it, realizing that it was a private restroom instead of one with multiple stalls, and closed and locked the door behind me before looking in the mirror.

What in the hell?

My face looked like I'd made out with a crayon. A really fucking bright crayon.

Reaching for a paper towel, I doused it with water and scrubbed at my face in vain. The bright color still remained in my facial hair and on my skin. Was I going to look like this forever?

Opening the door slowly, I peered outside to where April was standing guard. She saw me instantly and started shaking her head.

"Let me help," she demanded before pushing her way inside. "Figures that bitch would wear long-lasting lipstick," she said under her breath.

I had no idea what the hell she was talking about, but I was thankful that she—hopefully—knew how to get it off my face.

"Am I stuck like this?" I asked as she reached into her clutch and pulled out a tiny spray bottle.

Without saying a word, she soaked a paper towel and stepped toward me, her body so close to mine that my dick was aware of her nearness.

"I'm going to touch you now," she warned, her voice a little heady.

I inhaled as my dick grew harder. She was truly beautiful, and I'd been an asshole to pretend like she wasn't.

I watched as her hand moved toward my jaw, and she

started to rub at my skin gently. My eyes closed as a foreign sensation coursed through my veins. It wasn't unpleasant, but I couldn't quite place it.

"Am I hurting you?" she asked, misreading my body language completely.

"Not at all," I said as I covered her hand with my own, suddenly desperate to touch her. It was like I was seeing her for the first time.

Her eyes shot straight to mine with the contact, pinning me there. "Robbie." My name was an exhale, a request, a plea.

"April," I breathed out in equal measure.

"It's coming off," she said, and I hoped she meant her dress, but I wanted to smack myself when I realized she was talking about the lipstick.

She held up a pink paper towel, and when I glanced in the mirror, I saw that whatever was in her little bottle had done the trick.

"Thank you," I said, not moving my hand from hers.

When she tried to pull it away, I refused to let it go, and she kept it there.

This wasn't at all how I'd thought the night would turn out—getting overly excited about touching a girl's hand in some random restroom—but I wasn't complaining.

Hell, I wanted more.

IN A RESTROOM?!

APRIL

ROBBIE WAS CURRENTLY looking at me like I'd never been looked at before. His green eyes were practically glowing with desire. His mouth salivating. His dick still hard.

Yeah, I'd noticed the second it joined the party in the restroom. His hand was still covering mine, and even though I'd pretended to want to move it just moments before, I hadn't wanted to. Not really. Holding his jaw between my fingers was erotic. I didn't know how something so seemingly insignificant could elicit so much pleasure from my senses, but it did.

It had.

It still was.

"I'm going to kiss you now," Robbie said.

Before I could catch my next breath, his lips were on mine, his tongue sweeping across my lower lip in slow, delectable licks.

Oh good Lord in heaven, this man almost made my knees give out. His lips were soft and tasted like the facial mist I'd used to remove the lipstick stains. But even that didn't make me want to stop. He reached for my ass, his arms wrapping around me, and he lifted my body into the air and sat me on top of a piece of ornate furniture that, for whatever reason, was in this restroom.

I wanted to wrap my legs around him, but my dress was too long and too tight, and the only way to do that would be to push it all the way up to my goodies to get it out of the way. I wasn't ready for that. Unless he kept kissing me the way that he was. I might shred the damn thing into pieces just to get out of it. We were both adults. Sex didn't always have to equal life-altering moments and consequences.

One hand was at my neck, the other one on my thigh. I reached for his back, the muscles rippling against my fingertips as I pulled at his body. I wanted him nearer to me—nothing seemed close enough. I reached for his shirt, which was tucked into his pants, and started to pull at it when a hard knock on the door forced my heart to leap into my throat.

My hands dropped. His hands followed suit. Our lips parted. And he jumped about three feet away from me in that moment, turning his back to me as well.

"Hello? Is anyone in there, or do I need to have the door opened?" a voice asked.

Robbie cleared his throat loud enough for the person to hear.

"I'll be right out," he said, and the woman seemed satisfied with his response because she said nothing else.

When Robbie turned to face me again, the old him had returned. The one who didn't want to be here, who wasn't happy to see me and couldn't wait to get away. I could see it in his eyes. Shortly after the lipstick fiasco, when he had needed my help and was vulnerable, they had softened when he looked at me. But now, they were cold again.

He went to work, making himself presentable and attempting to tame the beast in his pants that anyone with eyes could spot from a mile away. I hopped off the piece of furniture I'd been sitting on and smoothed my dress, pulling it down before focusing on my makeup and hair in the mirror. Both looked like I'd just been screwed in a restroom.

"I shouldn't have done that," Robbie said, and it was like throwing a bucket of ice water all over my naked body.

"Me neither," I agreed even though I didn't agree. Not one single bit. But I refused to feel stupider than he was already making me feel.

"Guess I'll be in touch. Or something." He reached for the handle and pulled open the door right as someone walked in.

"Oh dear," she said before giving me a grin. "Oh dear!" she repeated, her tone like a verbal high five.

I couldn't believe I had been about to have sex with that asshole in a freaking restroom.

Where was April, and what had I done with her brain?

I WAS BACK at the office—my safe haven, the place where I could bury all thoughts of that stupidly hot fireman and pretend like he didn't star in my nightly fantasies. It had been almost a week since the auction, and while I was relieved that Robbie hadn't reached out, a part of me also couldn't stop overthinking, *Why hasn't he?*

"Has he called you yet?" Meredith asked, appearing out of thin air. Just like she'd asked me every day since I'd "won" the date with him.

"Nope," I said, hoping to sound completely unfazed and unbothered. Even though neither of those was entirely true.

"Do you want me to storm over to that firehouse and give him a piece of my mind?" She thrust her fists in the air and started punching.

I laughed. "Please don't. If he never calls, then this can all just go away, and I can focus on matching the couples who actually want my help."

"You know, April"—she jutted out her hip and smacked her lips together—"you can't do all the matching and never get matched yourself."

My smile dropped. I hated when people brought up my love life—or lack thereof—like it was something to be used against me.

I wasn't in the market for a relationship, and everyone

always acted like that was some kind of terrible mindset for me, of all people, to have. Like I was committing some horrific crime against humanity by denying myself love.

The truth was that I didn't feel like my life was currently lacking in any capacity. Work fulfilled me for the time being, but I wasn't naive enough to think that it would always be that way. I had enough self-awareness to realize that, at some point, I'd want a partner to share my time with. I just wasn't there yet.

Work demanded all of my attention, and I gave it willingly, happily, with a grateful and full heart.

My phone pinged out a notification from an unfamiliar number, and I hesitated before clicking on it. I was not in the habit of giving my personal cell to strangers, but I had an idea of who it might be.

Holding my cell in the air so Meredith could see it, I said, "I need to take this."

"Just think about what I said." She gave me a soft smile, almost like she felt bad for me.

I hated pity. Especially when it wasn't warranted.

"I heard you." I placated her because it really wasn't anyone's business what I decided to do with my heart and when.

Pressing on the unread text, I rolled my eyes as I read the message, knowing that it could only be from one person.

UNKNOWN: I'M DOING THIS UNDER DURESS. I AM LITERALLY BEING FORCED TO SEND YOU THIS RIGHT NOW.

Just as quickly as that message arrived, a picture came through. There stood Sheila with a fire hose aimed at Robbie, her hand poised over the lever that would turn it on and probably take his head clean off his shoulders. Those suckers were fierce.

ME: OKAY, YOU DID IT. YOU TEXTED ME. TELL SHEILA TO BACK OFF.

The three dots danced in the left corner before stopping and then reappearing as I begrudgingly added his phone number to my Contacts. It felt like the smart thing to do, considering there was no way in hell Sheila was going to let this go.

ROBBIE: YOU HAVE TO DO IT.

Letting out an annoyed *I don't have time for this* groan,

I quickly fired off a message to Sheila, telling her that Robbie had made contact and to put the hose down.

ROBBIE: THANK YOU. SHE'S A LITTLE INTENSE.

ME: AND SCARY. DON'T GET ON HER BAD SIDE.

I warned him even though it wasn't entirely true. Sheila wasn't scary; she was just pushy. She refused to give up when she had a thought or an idea. Like whatever it was she had conjured up in her mind about me and the fireman. She'd bought him as my date for a reason. One I couldn't quite fathom or even remotely understand.

ROBBIE: IS IT OKAY IF I CALL YOU LATER?

ME: SURE.

I stared at the screen of my phone, waiting to see if he'd say anything else but nothing came. The dots never started dancing, so there were no thoughts he wanted to share but quickly took back. He was gone as quickly as he'd appeared. And I wasn't sure how I felt about it.

GET THIS DATE OVER WITH

ROBBIE

APPARENTLY, I'D BROKEN some unspoken rule. Or hell, maybe it had been clearly written down, printed in black and white, and I'd ignored it. Too much time had passed since the night of the auction. At least, that was what Sheila implied when she stopped by the firehouse today, unannounced, looking for me, a stern expression on her face.

I needed to firm down an actual day for the date and inform the auction committee so that they could have everything in place. Including transportation. Limo, I'd been told. The over-the-top planning made me feel like I was back in high school, heading to prom.

Only I wasn't a seventeen-year-old virgin anymore, going solo with my guy friends, pretending like we were too cool to bring actual dates. I was a grown-ass adult now with a career and my own condo.

"Give me your phone," Sheila demanded before adding, "And don't even think about lying and telling me it's in your locker. I know it's in your pocket."

She pointed her finger right at my junk, and I begrudgingly pulled out my cell and gave it to her, wondering what she might do to embarrass me.

I watched as she moved her fingers across the screen before handing it back to me. "Start typing."

April's name was at the top of a new text message thread.

"I don't see your fingers moving." Sheila tsked at me before looking around the firehouse, like a snake searching for a field mouse. Her mouth twisted into a slight grin for only a split second before she slithered toward the fire truck and reached for the hose, unwinding it slowly.

"Darling," her voice practically purred.

My captain popped his head out from around the corner. "Yeah, babe?"

"This works, doesn't it?" she asked.

His eyes roved between the two of us, finally settling

back on her. "It works."

"Great." Sheila held it between her hands. Her long, manicured nails looked ridiculous against the dirty, mangled material. "Are you texting her, or do I need to give you a bath?"

It was official; this lady was insane.

My fingers started moving of their own accord, firing off a text before I snapped a picture of Sheila and sent that next. April responded right away, and I held my phone in Sheila's direction, so she could see.

"We're talking, okay? Look, she responded."

"Of course she did." Sheila grinned before setting the hose down gently on the ground and pulling her phone out of her purse, reading something. "I don't know how to put that back. Sorry." She waved toward the floor.

"I got it," I said because I knew that Captain would tell me to handle it the moment she left the premises.

"Such a sweet boy. Make sure you schedule that date. If the committee doesn't hear from you by end of day tomorrow, I'll be taking matters into my own hands."

It was a subtle warning, but a warning nonetheless. I had no idea what it all meant, but I did know that I didn't want Sheila McHenry taking anything of mine into her own hands.

With a nod toward Sheila, I finished texting April, letting her know that I'd call her later even though I wasn't sure that I would. Most likely, I'd forget. Not on purpose, but life at the firehouse was two things—either rambunctious or kind of boring.

In order to make sure I didn't unintentionally blow her off, I sent her one last text.

ME: MEET ME AT THE FIREHOUSE AFTER YOU GET OFF WORK?

I expected her to respond and be agreeable, not question me. So, when she replied with one single word and three question marks—WHY???—I found myself grinning despite my irritation.

ME: SO WE CAN PLAN THIS STUPID DATE. JUST COME HERE. IT WILL BE EASIER.

APRIL: EASIER FOR WHO?

ME: ME.

APRIL: SELFISH.

ME: NOT SELFISH. JUST HONEST. WILL IT HELP IF I SAY

PLEASE?

APRIL: IT WOULDN'T HURT.

ME: PLEASE.

APRIL: …

APRIL: …

APRIL: …

Whoever had invented those stupid dancing dots should be hurt. All they seemed to do was add more anxiety and stress to a situation, not ease it. I hated them. Knowing that someone was typing made my entire body tense up as I waited for whatever was about to be said in response. And when the dots disappeared and never returned, it was like sticking a knife in the side of my head.

What were they about to say? Why'd they stop typing?

APRIL: FINE. TEXT ME THE ADDRESS.

ME: I'LL DROP A PIN.

APRIL: I MIGHT BE LATE.

ME: I'LL BE HERE ALL NIGHT. IT DOESN'T MATTER.

APRIL: K.

K.

Girl code for, *Everything is not even remotely okay or anywhere close to it.*

April didn't want to come here, and honestly, I couldn't blame her. But the issue was, I couldn't go to her or meet her anywhere. At least, not for another thirty-six hours, and according to Sheila, I was already out of time. Being at the start of my shift, of which I lived and breathed at the firehouse, didn't leave me many options.

I guessed we could talk on the phone, but I had a feeling that before we did what we were supposed to, April would hang up on me. For some reason, we both seemed to push the other's buttons. I was sure it was mostly my fault, but I didn't want to participate in this farce. No matter how fucking sexy I found her. And trust me, she definitely turned me on, but I wasn't interested in dating right now.

Probably not ever, if I was being honest. And definitely not with a woman who went to bachelor auctions and actually bid on the men there. A woman like that couldn't be less my type. So why was I counting down the minutes until she showed up here, then?

OFF TO THE FIREHOUSE

APRIL

GLANCING AT THE time, I groaned, realizing that it was already close to eight p.m. I'd sent Meredith home a couple of hours ago, which wasn't unusual. I liked being in the office alone—when it was quiet and the lights started shutting themselves off because there was no movement to trigger them. The silence was soothing, especially considering the fact that this city was anything but.

Once I stepped outside of the building doors, I'd be greeted with the familiar sounds of horns honking, people shouting, and music blaring out of cars. The city itself seemed to hum with life, creating an undercurrent of noise that most tended to memorize without even meaning to.

My computer dinged out a calendar alarm, drawing my

attention to it. I'd set myself a notification that said, *Go see stupid Robbie at his stupid firehouse.* It was immature, but sometimes, I could be exactly that.

I fired off a text, letting him know that I was planning on heading over in a few minutes. If he had been called out to an emergency, I assumed that my message would go unread and unanswered. To my surprise, he responded right away and warned me that all the guys were still awake, playing cards.

Great.

Like seeing him at his *office* wasn't going to be awkward enough, but now, I'd be forced to meet all of his *coworkers* too, who I was sure had heard all kinds of things about me. Knowing Robbie, none of them would have been flattering.

Hailing a cab, I hopped in, gave the driver the address, pressed my back into the seat, and focused on my breathing. This wasn't a big deal. We'd pick a day to go on this date and get it over with. Then, we'd never have to see each other again. It would be like it never happened. Robbie, the hot fireman, would cease to exist in my universe, the same way he had two weeks ago.

And I'd be just fine with that.

"You meant to be dropped off here, correct?" the cab driver asked as he stopped in front of the firehouse.

How embarrassing. I was sure I looked like some sort of groupie or something. I wondered what the women who chased firemen were called.

"Yeah. Visiting my brother," I lied, but the look he gave me in his rearview let me know that he didn't believe me.

Why do I care what this person thinks about me?

Tossing him a twenty-dollar bill, I told him to keep the change as I exited the car and slammed the door shut harder than I'd meant to. He pulled away, and I stood outside of the brick building, the garage doors in front closed. It was only then that I realized I had no idea how to get inside. If the giant doors had been open, I would have walked right in and figured it out from there, but they weren't.

Pulling out my phone, I let Robbie know I was here and asked him where to go. Within seconds, one of the doors was swinging upward, the lights from inside turning the driveway from night to day.

Robbie appeared, a large silhouette at first before he turned three-dimensional. “Hey,” he said, and I tried not to ogle him.

I remembered how well that had gone over last time, but, damn, he was in uniform, and it looked tailor-made for his body. I understood the appeal. Not that I hadn’t before, but this man, decked out from head to toe in his dark blues, was a sight.

“Hey,” I said back, taking a few steps toward him. I wasn’t sure if we were just going to have a quick chat out here and I’d be on my way or if he had something else in mind.

“Come inside,” he directed, expecting me to follow him.

And I did. I mean, of course I did.

The first thing I noticed was how clean and organized it all was. Everything was in its proper place—I assumed. Boots were neatly stacked in front of hanging jackets on hooks. The fire truck was sparkling so bright that it looked like it belonged in a museum. I heard laughing echoing from somewhere, but no one was in my view as I looked around for the source.

Robbie was ahead of me, walking fairly fast as the garage closed behind me, but I kept up. He walked up three concrete steps before making a left and then another quick right. I did the same and was greeted by the smiling faces of four guys sitting around a round table. The room was like a large family room with a full-size kitchen and multiple couches. It looked comfortable, homey even.

"Everyone, this is April. April, this is everyone," Robbie said.

I found myself feeling slightly offended. He thought so little of me that I didn't even deserve a proper introduction with actual names.

"Hi, everyone," I repeated the term with slight distaste, so Robbie would know I was miffed.

He didn't seem to care though as he took a seat back at the table and grabbed the cards that had been facedown.

"I thought you two had business to discuss?" one of the men said, and I wanted to thank him for attempting to keep Robbie focused on the matter at hand.

I hadn't come here to watch a bunch of men play poker. No matter how hot they all were. And while I was sure that there were worse ways to spend an evening, I would have rather been at home, watching bad reality TV and unwinding from my long day before I woke up and repeated it all again tomorrow.

When I cleared my throat, the entire table focused on me, and I felt myself flush with embarrassment at their stares.

"Robbie"—my voice was quieter than I'd meant—"I do need to get home, so if we could get this over with . . ."

"See?" another guy with a bushy mustache said before adding, "She doesn't want to go out with you either. Although, personally, I think you're an idiot. Look at her. She's way out of your league."

Everyone started nodding and voicing their agreement. Everyone, except Robbie, who was glaring daggers at me. His dirty looks were starting to get on my nerves. I'd done nothing to deserve them.

"I'll take you out instead!" Mustache Man shouted, and I tried to hide my smile.

The chair Robbie sat in screeched against the concrete as he pushed it back, and my grin dropped instantly.

"Enough. You," he said, pointing a finger at me, "come with me."

My mouth twisted into a frown at his demand. He was so damn rude. Yet I followed him out of the living room and into a hallway.

"You're a jerk," I said loud enough for the rest of the guys to hear, and they started howling with laughter. I felt vindicated.

Robbie stopped walking abruptly for only a second before starting up again. "Yeah, I know."

"You're making this so much harder than it needs to be," I shouted at his back, once again following him around the fire station to who knew where.

We walked upstairs, and my eyes focused on the framed photographs of smiling faces that followed. They were tributes to the men they'd lost over the years. Of course, the majority had passed on 9/11, and my heart ached as I remembered what the city had been like during that time. I had only been a young kid when it happened, but a tragedy like that etched itself into your DNA. I'd never forget the way everyone had seemed to wear their pain like a thunder storm, loud and palpable, refusing to be ignored.

When we reached the top, there were a couple of doors

to what I'd soon learn were bedrooms. We stepped into one room, multiple twin beds all sharing the space, and I shuddered at the sheer lack of privacy. It reminded me of the dorm rooms back in college. Robbie stopped at the foot of one of the beds before sitting on it. I looked around, unsure of what to do, so I sat on the empty bed next to his.

"Not much privacy," I practically whispered, and Robbie's green eyes shot up to meet mine.

"None. You can't do anything here without someone hearing you."

He was opening up. It was a small thing, but it was more than he'd given me up until this point.

"Is it annoying?" I asked. "Or are you used to it?"

His head shook slowly. "You never really get used to it."

I wasn't sure what to say in response to that. Even though I wanted to keep him talking, I found myself struggling to find a topic.

"So …" I stumbled on what I wanted to ask exactly.

"Soooo," he repeated, dragging out the word in an irritated tone.

"Why do you do that?" I snarled, folding my arms

across my chest, and I watched his eyes follow the movement.

"Do what?"

"Act like you hate me."

"I don't know." He closed his eyes before opening them again, a long breath leaving his chest. "I don't hate you. It's just"—he paused before continuing—"this whole situation makes me uncomfortable."

It felt like the first honest thing he'd said to me since we'd met.

"So, your defense mechanism is to be a dick?"

He let out a slight laugh that almost made me smile in response. "I guess. I've never realized it, but, yeah, I probably do act like that."

"Trust me, you do," I said, my tone light instead of accusatory.

He angled his body toward me, his arms bearing the weight as he leaned into them. "Why do you think your girl Sheila is pushing this so hard?"

That truly was the million-dollar question. The one thing I hadn't been able to figure out.

"I honestly don't know," I said before blowing out a

loud sigh that caused him to give me a questioning look.

"I feel like you might know something." He suddenly looked interested, like I might be hiding information that he needed.

I shook my head. "No, it's just that, sometimes, she sees things."

"Sees things?" he asked. "Like a psychic? What do you mean? Elaborate, please."

Oh, he said please. That's a first.

"She just sees things that other people can't." As soon as I said the words, I realized how cuckoo I sounded. Like maybe I was talking about her being a psychic or having some other kind of New Age abilities.

"Like what?"

He was getting the wrong impression.

"You know what she used to do for a living, right? What I do for work?"

His eyes pulled together, causing little creases to form in his skin. "Actually, no. I have no idea."

How could he not know this?

"Really? You don't know anything? Your fire captain didn't tell you? You know they're dating, right?"

He shifted on the bed, sitting up straight, his hands resting in his lap. "I don't know anything. No one has told me shit. So, if you'd care to fill me in, that'd be great."

I put my hands in the air. "Don't get mad." I tried to sound reasonable and calming. I liked the version of him that wasn't pissed off twenty-four/seven much better than the constantly bitter one.

"Sorry," he said, and I felt like he actually meant it.

"Anyway, Sheila was my mentor. She owned the business before she sold it to me. I'm a matchmaker."

A loud laugh escaped him, followed by another, echoing in the space between us, and before I knew it, he was cracking up. "You're joking, right?"

My hackles started to rise as I felt myself getting defensive. It seemed like he was laughing *at* me. "Why would I be joking?"

Once he calmed down and could actually talk without chuckling, he managed to say, "I guess I didn't realize that those places still existed. Like real-life matchmakers? Setting people up on dates and stuff?"

"Why is that so hard to believe?"

"There are a hundred dating sites online," he started

explaining, as if I didn't know this already. "Everyone I know has at least one on their phone."

"Do you?" I asked bitterly, realizing that I wanted him to tell me no. Something in me didn't want Robbie to be the kind of guy who had an online dating profile.

"Definitely not me."

I felt my chest literally sigh with relief, although I wasn't entirely sure why. It wasn't like he was overly nice to me or even acted like he was interested in me.

"Well, those sites are all filled with the exact same people. My clients get tired of seeing the same faces over and over again. They're looking for something more genuine, someone who wants what they want. And they don't think they can find that online. They've tried."

Robbie pushed up from the bed and made his way across to where I was sitting. He sat down next to me, his leg touching mine. "I can see the appeal in that."

"Gee, thanks."

"I'm not trying to offend you." He sounded so defeated.

I forced a fake smile. "Yet here we are."

Out of nowhere, the fire alarms started blaring, scaring

the ever-loving crap out of me. Robbie looked at me, his eyes wide, like this was the last thing he'd expected, and he jumped up.

"I have to go. I'll call you later."

"We haven't even picked a date yet," I shouted, like any of that truly mattered in a moment like this.

"I'm off on Friday. Let's do it then," he said before disappearing.

I ran after him, watching as he slid down the pole I hadn't even noticed before. The guys below moved like a well-rehearsed dance, pulling on their boots, fastening their jackets, and hopping onto the fire truck before it pulled out of the garage, sirens wailing.

And just like that, I was alone. I sat there, dumbfounded at how quickly it had all happened. And a little scared, if I was being honest. It was in that moment that the force of what Robbie did for work really hit me. Of course, I had known he was a fireman, but seeing him in action, knowing that he was heading toward something that could potentially hurt him ... *rattled me.*

Every single time he left the safety of this station and got onto that truck, there was a possibility that he might not come back. *Ever.* The walls were a stark reminder of that fact. And with every frantic beat, my heart was letting me know that it didn't want anything bad to happen to him.

I fired off a text, asking Robbie to call me when he got back from wherever he'd gone to, regardless of the time. I wasn't going to be able to sleep without knowing that he was okay.

That should have been my first clue that I had something resembling actual feelings for the guy … *but it wasn't.* Apparently, I was good at lying to myself and pretending like any sane person would want to make sure that he was okay under the circumstances.

I also convinced myself that it was completely normal to sit, staring at the phone until it rang with his name on the screen.

What if it never did again?

OBLIGATION OR SOMETHING MORE

ROBBIE

I CALLED APRIL that night after I got back to the firehouse and showered, like she'd asked me to in a text message. Trust me, I almost hadn't. But she sounded so relieved to hear from me when she answered on the first ring that my heart honestly felt like it leaped in my chest and spun the fuck around.

The idea that she might have been worried about my well-being and safety while I was on the job was such a foreign notion that I couldn't even work up the nerve to ask her about it. I couldn't take being wrong. The thought alone was nice enough without making her say it out loud. Could she really care about me?

I hadn't felt valued or worthy of love in what seemed

like forever. Maybe I never truly had. My parents didn't count. I was so used to feeling mistreated by women that the idea of April actually giving a shit about me had never even crossed my mind.

So, when I hung up the phone, I had an unfamiliar feeling in the pit of my stomach. I wasn't sure what it meant, so I tried my best to ignore it and pretend like it wasn't there. I figured it would dissipate while I slept and be gone by the time I woke up. If it didn't, I'd chalk it up to nerves. What else could it be?

I SAT IN the back of the limo, feeling like an idiot as we cruised up Seventh Avenue toward what I assumed would be April's residence. Only we didn't stop in front of an apartment building at all.

She's having me pick her up at her office?

I forgot that most people didn't have Fridays off of work, so this actually made sense. Even if it was a little late in the evening, of course April would still be here. As I stifled a slight laugh at my little workaholic, it caught in my throat at the sight of her walking out of the revolving glass door.

Hell, I almost started choking on it. Her *leave nothing to the imagination* white dress made visions of her in another white dress flash in my mind. Closing my eyes and shaking my head to rid myself of the thought, I reopened them, so I wouldn't miss a second of her. I wasn't the only one who noticed, and a possessive streak I hadn't even known I had roared to life. Other men were watching my date, salivating at the sight of her, thinking they had a chance.

Fuck. No.

Without thinking twice, I exited the car and made my way toward her. Every guy in the vicinity needed to know that she wasn't available. At least, not tonight. She looked genuinely surprised by my actions, her eyes meeting mine and holding. They sparkled in the fading sunlight, enraptured by every step I took closer to her body.

When I finally reached her, my hand cupped her cheek before I ran a knuckle down the length of it. Her skin was as soft as it appeared. It took everything in me not to take her in my arms and kiss her senseless. Something about it felt so natural in the moment. It wasn't as if I hadn't kissed her before.

"You look beautiful," I said, watching how the compliment made her turn red. Or maybe it was my touch. I couldn't be sure which one had caused her reaction, but I knew how much I fucking loved it.

"Thank you. You look quite dashing yourself," she said.

I smirked at her word choice. I liked it.

I pulled her hand into mine, intertwining our fingers as we glided across the busy sidewalk toward the limo. I tried not to pay attention to the whistles that rang out around us, no doubt directed toward April, but it was difficult. I wanted to knock out every guy who so much as looked at her in that dress even if it was a passing glance.

"This car is stupid," she said, breaking me from the spell I had been under.

"Tell me about it," I agreed as I helped her inside and quickly followed behind.

"Going to Tavern on the Green for a first date is stupid too," she added.

A deep laugh escaped from my chest. "I want to argue with you, but I can't."

Our bodies both got shoved into the back cushions as the driver stepped on the gas and headed into traffic without warning, offering a quick sorry in response.

"Of course you want to argue."

Angling my legs toward hers, I pinned her with a smoldering look. At least, I hoped it appeared that way. The last thing I wanted was for April to think I was being a dick when I really wanted to devour her in every place she'd allow it. "What's that supposed to mean?"

Her tongue darted out to lick her lips, and another vision crashed into me without warning. Her naked body underneath mine, bending to my every whim, as cries of pleasure escaped from her mouth. I wanted to be the one making her scream as she came.

"I just meant that all you do is argue with me. You're not very agreeable."

Fantasy over.

I cleared my throat. "I literally just said I agreed with you about this car. And Tavern. Sounds pretty agreeable to me."

"You're not wrong." Her voice sweetened an octave. "Can I ask you something?"

"Sure." I shrugged a shoulder and waited.

A grin took over her face, and damn if I didn't want to be the one who made her smile. "If this was a real first date, where would we be going?"

Shit.

I hadn't expected that question. I hadn't even thought about anything other than the ridiculous parameters of this date. When was the last time I'd actually taken someone out and not just headed to their apartment for sex?

"Didn't think that would be such a difficult question," she teased, and I was relieved that she seemed less tense around me.

"I can't remember the last time I went on a date," I admitted, and she looked at me like I was lying.

"Oh, come on." Her tone was one hundred percent sarcastic. She didn't believe me.

"I mean it. I haven't been on a *date*, date in years."

"I find it hard to believe that a guy like you hasn't had sex in *years*," she said, emphasizing the length of time, and I let out a loud laugh.

"I never said that," I offered nonchalantly, like it wasn't a big deal even though it kind of was.

"Yeah, I guess you didn't. I just assumed. Sorry, that was stupid. Of course you could have sex without dating." She started talking fast, her words spilling out as quickly as the thoughts came to her head.

"And you?" I turned the tables.

That topic was a little too uncomfortable for me. The number of women I'd slept with over the years and never talked to again wasn't something I was proud of… *anymore*. It used to seem so cool, being the guy who could get any girl into bed. I'd worn it like a badge of honor, like I possessed some sort of magical power that no other guy could even come close to.

It wasn't cool anymore.

I wasn't proud.

And the worst part was, I couldn't take any of it back or make the number of sexual partners I'd had in my past go down. I only hoped April didn't ask for the number because I really didn't want to lie to her.

"I don't date," she said before adding, "And I don't usually have sex with random guys."

"You don't date? Why?" My curiosity was definitely piqued with this woman.

She was completely different than I'd thought she'd be. Her being at the bachelor auction had soured me toward her instantly. And I didn't really believe her when she said she'd only gone as a favor to Sheila. At the time, it didn't make any sense. I'd assumed that April was just like every other woman I'd met, looking for a fling, a one-night stand, or a hot guy to fuck and tell her friends about.

"I'm just really busy, you know? I've made work my priority for the time being."

"So, you help everyone else find love, except yourself. Is that what I'm hearing?" I was only joking, but I seemed to hit some sort of nerve.

The smile on her face dropped, and her eyes looked everywhere, except at mine, as her body stiffened. I wasn't even sure she knew how tense she'd just become.

"Why does everyone always say that?"

I reached out, my hand touching hers. I figured she'd pull it away, but she didn't.

"Hey. Look at me." I tried to sound comforting, but she refused to listen. "Look at me," I said even more stern this time.

Eventually, those hazel irises looked up and right into

my soul.

"I was only joking. It's okay with me if you want to work and find love later. I get it."

"Sorry. It's just that I hear that a lot, and it's so frustrating." She pulled her hand away from mine, and it took all of my willpower not to take it right back.

It was *my* hand now.

"Which part?"

"Huh?"

"Which part is frustrating?" I asked, hoping she'd clarify and give me another glimpse into her personality, which I was enjoying more than I'd expected to.

Her body visibly started to relax, and I felt myself exhale with relief. For some reason, I hated seeing her so upset. All I wanted to do was fix it.

"It's like no one believes me when I say that I'm not lonely. Or that I'm not looking for love. Or that I'm completely satisfied with my job," she explained, her chest heaving with each breath she took. "Why can't I be happy, just working? I'm the most successful matchmaker in Manhattan. That's a huge accomplishment. I've continued to build this incredible business. But that's not enough. I think it's because I'm a woman, so people expect me to want more."

I shook my head slowly as her thoughts soaked into my mind, and I felt like I understood her. "I think you're right."

She let out a fake laugh. "About what?"

"It's totally because you're a woman. We've been conditioned since birth, you know? You're not allowed to be successful *and not* want a family." I spoke the words like it was the most asinine thought in the world … because it kind of was. All outdated and old-fashioned.

"I do want a family though. I want a husband. Kids. All of it." She spoke softly. Her hand moved to rest on my thigh, and I tried to stay focused on what she was saying instead of where she was touching me. "Just not yet."

In that moment, a thought hit me so hard that it was almost violent. I knew that the message was as much for me as it was for her, hence the gravity of it.

"Because you haven't met the right person yet," I whispered, almost to myself, but she heard me.

"Excuse me?"

"You want all of those things in the future because you

haven't met anyone who makes you want them now."

April stayed quiet, her lips pulled together tight, and I wondered if I'd just ruined the whole evening before it even got to begin. "I never thought about it that way before."

Start thinking about it, sweetheart, was what I wanted to say but didn't.

Doing so would have forced us to delve into a conversation that I wasn't sure I was ready to have or could admit to just yet. Our eyes were locked on to one another's, both of us trying to read what the other one refused to say out loud. That there was something here between us.

"What about you, Mr. I Have Sex But I Don't Date?"

I choked a little on the air around us. "What about me, what?"

"Haven't met the right woman yet?"

"Not looking," I lied because I was looking right fucking at her. And somewhere deep inside me, I knew it.

"Why not? Too many options for you to settle on just one?" She asked the question with a smile, but her tone bordered on disgusted.

April didn't want my answer to be yes.

"I'm going to tell you something," I said.

She sat up straighter as she gave me her full attention. "I'm ready."

"I don't think women like me very much." It wasn't what I'd meant to say or how I'd meant to say it, but it was what had come out when I opened my mouth.

April's head tilted to one side, her eyes narrowing. "I thought you were going to be serious."

"I am being serious." I huffed out a breath. "The women I meet …" I stopped for a second. "They don't care about me. They want to screw the hot fireman from the calendar and never talk to me again." I tried to sound as matter-of-fact as possible, without any emotion, but I wasn't sure I'd succeeded.

Searching April's face for any signs of understanding, I waited for her to say something … anything that might make me feel a little less tore open and vulnerable.

"What calendar?" she asked, and I instantly regretted bringing it up.

The damn thing had ruined me and turned me into the kind of guy who *complained* about getting laid.

"You know, the yearly firemen calendar? It's a fundraiser."

She shook her head. "Ohhh, yeah. I mean, I've never seen one, but I've heard about them. So, you were in it?"

"I was in it. On the cover actually."

"And the women …" she started to say, but her upper lip curled up into a small snarl that was downright adorable. "What did they do?"

I could tell by April's tone that she didn't like this part of my story. Her arms tensed as she braced for my answer, her hands making little fists, like she wanted to fight for my honor. She hated that I felt mistreated. Even if she never admitted it, her body language gave her away.

"Chased me. Reached out to me in every possible way. At first, it was flattering. I thought I might actually meet someone and fall in love, but I learned pretty quickly that it wasn't going to be like that. All the DMs, the comments on my social media accounts, the calls to the firehouse—they were all just looking to hook up. Nothing more. No one wanted to go on an actual date or get to know me. They literally just wanted to have sex."

"I'm sorry." She put up a hand with an awkward grin

on her face. "It's just that I've never heard a guy talk like this before. Actually complain about women just wanting sex with them instead of a relationship."

I groaned. "I know. Trust me, I know. Do you have any idea how shitty it feels to be used? Like you're not worthy of actual love?"

It was a question I hadn't meant to ask. It was more rhetorical than anything else, but she opened her mouth to answer anyway.

"Of course I know what it's like to feel used. I'm a woman. The shoe is usually on our foot." She was stating the obvious. "But it's kind of refreshing to hear someone like you say all of that."

"Someone like me?"

"Yeah. Hot. Successful. Kind of nice—when you're not busy being a jerk."

That made me laugh. And the laughter gave me a break from all the heaviness I had been spilling out to her. So, I did what I seemed to do best and changed the subject … *again*.

"Do you like any of the things on our date?"

"Wait, what?"

It was like I'd given her emotional whiplash, moving from one topic to another abruptly and without warning, but it was the only way I could refocus my own brain and get it back on track.

Otherwise, the next words out of my mouth were going to be me confessing to this woman that I was falling for her and there wasn't a damn thing she could do about it. But I was not in a good place to have her reject me, so I had to keep my mouth shut.

DESSERT FOR DINNER

APRIL

ROBBIE WAS A master subject changer. I was sure he thought he was slick about it, but he wasn't. He was obvious. Getting a little uncomfortable or things getting a little too real … and cue the subject change.

I could have called him out on it, but he'd touched on something that I'd tried to ignore, something I'd done my best not to breathe much life into even though it had been simmering in the back of my mind since the night we had first met.

I had feelings for him.

And the way he had just opened up to me was like seeing him in a whole new light. A room filled with so much brightness that I needed to squint to look at him head-on. I wasn't sure if what I was feeling for him was truly real, had any kind of lasting potential, or if it was just a passing fancy brought on by what he'd just shared with me, but regardless, there were strong emotions bubbling just underneath the surface. If he scratched too hard, it would all come pouring out and drown us both.

"All the things that we're supposed to do tonight—do you like any of them?" Robbie continued with the new topic of conversation, and I tried to keep up even though my mind kept replaying him saying how he felt used and unworthy of love.

This gorgeous man didn't think he was worth loving.

"Oh." I shook my head as it clicked into place what he was asking. "Well, I'm not opposed to Serendipity. This girl loves a good frozen hot chocolate. But I could really take or leave the rest. What about you?"

"Tavern seems a bit much. So serious, you know? I don't ice-skate, and I really don't want to. The last thing I need is to get hurt doing something like that and not be able to work while I recover. I'd be miserable."

I hadn't even thought about that before. The fact that, if he got hurt, it would stop him from helping others. If anything happened to me, I could still hobble into the office and sit behind my desk all day, making matches from the comfort of my oversize chair. My life wouldn't change if I broke an ankle, but Robbie's would be put on hold.

"That makes sense. I didn't even think about that. Sorry." I felt like a jerk for not even processing the severity of his job and how much it meant to him.

"Nothing to be sorry about. But, hey, I'm always down for dessert," he said before he looked straight into my lap, and I felt myself flush.

Was he flirting? Was he not? I hated that I couldn't tell.

I bit my bottom lip, taking it between my teeth as I smiled, deciding to push my luck. "Are you thinking what I'm thinking?"

His face paled slightly but enough that I noticed. I felt stupid that he was definitely not thinking what I was, so I tried to recover and play it off.

"Dessert for dinner?" I asked, my tone insecure, my words a little shaky.

His face returned to its normal color. "I'm definitely down with that."

"I'm a little overdressed." I looked at my outfit before running a hand across my flat stomach. I'd barely eaten all day, knowing that I'd most likely overindulge this evening.

"You could take it off," he blurted out, leaving me more confused than I had been seconds ago.

"Then, I wouldn't be dressed at all," I fired back, daring him to say more.

Had I misread all the signs I thought he'd been giving me since he'd stormed out of the limo and appeared at my side, all fire and lust in his eyes? The look on his face reminded me of our moment in the restroom the night of the auction. He had wanted me then. Before we were interrupted. I knew he had.

I was definitely rusty when it came to picking up on social cues when it came to myself. For other people, I could read them like a book regardless of how they tried to act or what words they said. But for me, it wasn't as easy. I had no idea what Robbie was thinking, what he wanted, or how he felt about me.

"April …" Robbie said my name in a breath, forcing me to ignore my inner dialogue and give him my full attention.

"Yes?"

"You look fucking stunning. I'm afraid I might kill every guy who even looks at you tonight."

I was sure that should have been a turn-off, his possessive alpha words, but the way he'd said it, all raw and honest, was so flipping hot that I was anything but turned off. Plus, I was sure that he wouldn't really *kill* anyone. It was just something people said. An exaggerated phrase with no real threat behind it.

"I do have a jacket," I said, showing him the long white coat that I had sitting next to me that he clearly hadn't seen before.

"Put that on. Right now."

I started laughing even though I knew he wasn't joking. He wanted me to cover myself up, just like I'd hoped he would when I got ready at the office earlier. It had been part of my plan to *wow* him this evening. I chose this particular dress for that exact reason. I knew how I looked in it, and I'd wanted Robbie to come undone when he saw me.

"Driver, change of plans," Robbie shouted, and the

driver met his gaze in the rearview mirror. "Just take us straight to Serendipity."

He started shaking his head slowly. "Can't do that, sir. Miss Sheila will have my ass if I deviate from the plan."

Just as I went to pull my phone out of the clutch I'd brought with me, Robbie's strong hands stopped me. He gave me a small shake of his head, and I knew that he had some kind of strategy in mind. I decided to trust him right as the driver informed us that we had arrived at our destination before pulling to a complete stop.

The two of us waited in the back for him to open our door, and Robbie exited first before helping me out. Such a gentleman when he wanted to be.

"The jacket, sweetheart," he practically purred.

I melted a little inside at the nickname. That little bit of softness that he allowed me to see only made me want more of it.

"Put it on." His green eyes burned with the request.

"Fine." I did so without complaint. I was going to put it on before he even told me to. It was cold as hell outside, but I wasn't going to admit that to him.

"I'll be parked at the structure up the street. Just call

me after you're done at Wollman." Our driver handed Robbie a business card, and before I could say anything, Robbie faced me and shot me a look that told me to keep my mouth shut.

"I'll text you," Robbie said.

The driver looked a little defeated, like the use of texting technology made him sad but accepted it with a sharp nod. "Have a nice time."

"We will, thank you," I said before he disappeared back into the car and pulled away.

I turned on my heel and faced Robbie, one hand on my hip. "I thought you had a plan!" I shouted before realizing that people were already watching us. Our clothes and the fact that we'd arrived in a limo had us attracting unwanted attention.

Robbie's arm gripped my waist as he pulled me close. "I do. It involves us leaving."

"Leaving?" I questioned, and his hand was on my face again, holding me steady as his thumb traced my jawbone.

I tried to swallow, but my throat felt like it had closed right up with his touch. God, I wanted this man to kiss me like he had in the restroom that night. But I knew I wouldn't want him to stop once he started.

"Yeah. Blowing this off. And Wollman. I'm not putting on those skates."

His tone let me know that there would be no negotiation about the ice-skating—not that I wanted to do it anyway, so he'd get no argument from me. Plus, how could he think I would encourage us to do something that might get him hurt? I would never do that.

"All right then, where are we headed?" I asked.

A grin appeared, and it made me do the same. Seeing him smile was like being given a gift, and I never wanted to stop unwrapping it.

"I'm going to kiss you," he said, catching me completely off guard. Not because I didn't want him to. Oh, how I did. But because I wasn't sure that he wanted me as much as I wanted him.

"It's about damn time," I said before his lips met mine, not crashing the way I'd thought they would, but tenderly and with care.

His movements were slow, his lips savoring every part that they touched. He devoured my mouth, his tongue making its way inside with purpose, like he was memorizing every inch of me.

His hand snaked its way through my coat and onto my ass. He gripped me there, a moan escaping me as my body leaned into him of its own volition. I couldn't remember the last time I'd been so turned on. My entire being felt like it was on fire, and it definitely did not want to be put out.

This fireman needed to let me burn for him.

SHE WAS ONTO SOMETHING

ROBBIE

FUCK FROZEN HOT chocolate or any dessert that wasn't April laid out beneath me on my king-size bed.

"I want to get out of here," I said before thinking about the consequences or what it all might mean after the fact. I had just admitted to her that I felt used for sex in the past, that women didn't want anything more than that from me, and here I was, propositioning her.

"Please."

It was all the permission I needed. "I can't call our driver."

"We can take the train," she suggested.

I gave her a once-over. She might have brought a jacket, but it still hugged her body like a second dress, none of her curves hidden at all underneath it.

Her body had been made to torture me.

"I can't take public transportation with you looking like that," I said.

She glanced down at herself. "I'm wearing a jacket."

"That's not a jacket. I don't even know what this is." I picked at the sleeve before dropping it. "It's attached to you." She started giggling, and I frowned. "You did this on purpose. Didn't you?"

Stepping closer, I grabbed her body with my hands and held on tight. This was the beginning of me never letting her go, whether she realized it or not. Leaning down, I claimed her mouth once more.

It was *my* mouth.

I ran my hands down the curves of her waist to her hips before landing on her thighs.

Mine.

Moving my hands higher I gripped her ass, holding it tight.

All. Fucking. Mine.

This woman would be my complete undoing, but what a way to go.

"You've got to stop touching me like that," she

breathed out.

I hadn't even considered what my touch was doing to her. I only knew what it did to me.

"Why's that?" I asked, teasing, toying, wanting to hear her tell me the way I made her feel with details I could never unhear.

" 'Cause if you don't, I'm going to forget that we're in public and let you have your way with me." Her voice was breathless, her tone ragged, as her hands gripped the waist of my pants.

"I'd never let anyone else see you the way I'm about to." I tried to speak calmly, but the words came out in a possessive growl. "I won't share you, April."

I'd never thought about any female like that before. Years ago, I wouldn't have cared if another man saw a girl I was with naked. I would have shown the dirty pictures she'd texted me to the guys at the firehouse. I realized that made me a certain kind of asshole, but, ladies, don't text naked pictures to men who don't love you. There's a ninety-nine percent chance that they'll eventually show them to *someone* … if not a lot of someones.

But not April. The idea that some other man might

touch her, kiss her, or look at her the way I was about to made me fucking crazy. I couldn't even think about it without wanting to tear my mind out. She was for my eyes only.

"I won't share you either, Robbie. I can't. Please don't ask me to." Her voice was so sincere that it almost stopped my heart from beating.

No woman had ever said that to me before. They never cared what I did or with who.

"I never would."

"Then, take me home."

Her eyes sparked with emotion, and she looked at me like no one ever had before. April's eyes told me that this wasn't just for one night; this was bordering on serious, maybe even love.

A man who wasn't ready would have run from that look.

I wanted more of it.

MY APARTMENT WAS only a twenty-minute cab ride away, but it felt like an eternity. April was pressed up against me, my hand tightly holding hers in case she tried to open the door and hop out. I wasn't letting her get away, and I prayed that she didn't come to her senses on the drive back to my place and question what the hell she was doing, going home with me.

"My apartment was closer," April said as she watched us cruise past Twenty-Fifth Avenue.

"You live on Twenty-Fifth?" I asked, assuming that was why she'd mentioned it.

"Twenty-Ninth and Sixth," she offered.

I grinned inwardly. That was pretty specific, and she knew that I'd be able to at least narrow down the buildings if I had to. Hopefully, it wouldn't come to that, and she'd invite me over willingly.

"We're almost to my place," I said, hoping it would calm her down.

I'd gotten a really great deal for being a firefighter at an older community that had been recently taken over and updated. It had a *suburban neighborhood* feel to it. And even though I wasn't home that often, I loved it when I was.

The driver pulled to a stop, and I shoved my credit

card into the seat reader before leaving a twenty percent tip and telling him thanks.

"Do you think we should have told our limo driver that we left?" April asked as we exited, and she glanced around at the grounds. "It's really pretty here. They did a great job, updating the grounds."

"You remember what it used to look like?" I asked because it had really been run-down at one point and hadn't been considered a safe place to reside.

She nodded her head. "I do. The buildings look the same though, which I think is nice."

"Until you walk inside," I said before holding my phone as tightly with one hand as I was holding her with the other. "Do you want me to text our driver and tell him we took off?"

"I think it's the polite thing to do. Don't you?"

"I don't know," I admitted as I pulled her toward one of the tall brick buildings. "I'm afraid he might show up here and pull us out by our feet, kicking and screaming, at Sheila's request."

April started laughing. "You're not wrong. But we should still tell him," she added before snapping her fingers together. "Oh! I know! Tell him I got sick and we took a cab home. There was no time to wait. Didn't want to vomit in his car and leave him with that mess to clean up." She kept explaining all about her fake illness, and I had to admit, it was a good plan.

"I'm doing that. Saying all of that. So, if Sheila asks you, you'd better go with it."

She let go of my hand and slapped her palm against her forehead. "Ugh. Knowing her, she'll make us go on the date all over again."

"Does the woman have no Off button?" I asked absentmindedly as I typed as quickly as my fingers would allow.

April shook her head. "Not when she has an idea in her mind."

Pressing Send on the text, I waited to see that the message was delivered. I got an immediate response. "He said okay and he hopes you feel better and that he still would have taken you home."

"Of course he would have. It's his job. Tell him thank you again and that I'll talk to Sheila."

I did as she'd asked, typing out her message word for

word so that the driver would hopefully get a sense of relief instead of thinking he'd get in trouble, before I pocketed my phone.

"It's right here." I nodded toward the brick building on the left.

I scanned my key fob across the pad at the entrance and held the door open for April as soon as it unlocked with a loud click.

"Elevators are up ahead. I'm on the tenth floor."

She looked around at the hallway we walked down, her eyes taking in all of the artwork that lined the walls. When we reached the elevators, she pressed the Up button before I could do it.

The doors opened, and I followed her as she stepped inside. Reaching around her body, I pushed the button for the tenth floor and didn't miss the way her breath skipped at my closeness.

"You know," I whispered near her ear and watched as her eyes closed in response, "we never did finish our conversation about Sheila."

April immediately tensed, her shoulders moving up a full inch as her hazel eyes shot back open and met mine.

"The one where you said she *sees things*."

The way I'd said it made her smile, and she swatted my shoulder playfully.

"I only meant that she has a knack for bringing couples together. She sees it before they do."

"How?"

"I don't know." April sounded exasperated. "I've asked her a thousand times, and she always just shrugs her shoulders and says she can't explain it. She says it's a feeling she gets."

"Do you get that feeling too? With your couples?" I wondered if it was something that perfected itself with time or if there was more to it than that. Was this some sort of ability, or did it come with the territory and familiarity of the job?

"It's only happened twice."

"Were you right?"

She smiled and nodded. "Yeah."

"So, is that what Sheila's doing here?" I wagged a finger between our two bodies. "Between us?"

The elevator came to a stop as April looked at me, unsure of how to answer.

"I think so. But to be fair—" she started to explain, but I pulled her out as soon as the doors opened and held her against me. She was so short compared to me, even in her heels, and I liked the way her head rested perfectly on my chest. She stopped talking completely, her body melting into mine.

"Keep going," I encouraged before giving her a soft kiss.

April cleared her throat and looked away from me, like she needed to do that in order to focus. And I understood completely. Looking at her and trying to make sense of any thoughts I had in my head at the same time was a fucking task.

"I was saying, to be fair, I think she was onto something."

"I couldn't agree more."

JUMPING THE GUN

APRIL

I TRULY NEVER saw this coming. Me and Robbie, the grumpy firefighter who, before tonight, had always seemed to be in a perpetually bad mood. The fact that I was walking hand in hand toward the front door of his apartment to most likely—no, definitely—have sex with him was something I could have never foreseen.

The night of the bachelor auction felt like it had been a million years ago even though it had only been a few weeks at most. He'd been such a jerk then. And he still was sometimes. But behind that rough exterior was a guy with an aching heart. Someone who had been hurt over and over again.

Under the surface of this hot-as-hell fireman was a man who felt like he wasn't worth loving.

I planned on showing him just how worthy he was.

We walked through his front door, and I stopped myself from gasping at how clean his place was. It had to be his occupation. All the strict rules for keeping the firehouse organized spilled over into his home life. Which, trust me, I was not complaining about. Men could be slobs. How nice it would be to live with someone who wasn't.

LIVE WITH SOMEONE? Slow down, cowgirl.

"It's not much, I know," he started to say, and I wasn't sure what he meant at first before I realized that he lived in a studio and not a one-bedroom.

Did he really think I cared about that? This was Manhattan after all. Living here was expensive.

"But I'm only here half the time," he added.

"It's perfect. What more do you need?" I asked with a smile. "And, yeah, what is your schedule like?"

"I'm usually on for one day and off for two. But sometimes it varies. And if there's a major incident on my off day, I go in."

"What does that mean exactly? The on part?" I had a general idea of firemen from movies and stuff, but I didn't know what was reality or what was exaggerated for the sake of entertainment.

"It means, I sleep at the firehouse. I live there for twenty-four at a time." He walked into the kitchen before asking me if I wanted something to drink.

"Water would be great actually," I said before sitting down on one of the two barstools.

He grabbed two glasses before opening the fridge and pulling out a pitcher filled with filtered water. I had the exact same one at my place. He slid one of the glasses across the kitchen island toward me, and I took it, our fingers brushing, sending chills racing down my spine. Robbie stayed across the island, and I wasn't sure if he was using it as a buffer in order to keep his distance from me or if he thought that my feelings had somehow changed in the last ten minutes so he was giving me space.

"When I say that I live at the firehouse for twenty-four hours, I mean it. I can't leave. Or spend the night anywhere else. I'm on call every minute of every hour while I'm there."

Realization smacked me upside the head. This was another one of his defense mechanisms. The more he revealed to me about his lifestyle, the more worried he was that I might not accept it.

"I get it."

"Do you?"

"Yes." I tried to reassure him. "I mean, obviously, I don't know what it's like yet, and I'm sure there will be days when I wish you could come stay with me instead of your fire bros, but I work a lot, too, so I think we'll be okay."

His mouth twisted up into a grin as everything I'd just said replayed in my mind. I'd basically jumped the gun and said we were dating before the man even told me he wanted anything to do with me after this night.

He pushed off the counter with both arms and stalked toward me. I watched his every move, my eyes locked on to his. When he reached me, he spun the barstool and positioned himself between my legs, his arms outstretched around me, securing me in place.

"You want this?" he asked, and I had no idea what *this* he was referring to.

"Which *this* are you talking about exactly?"

"All of it. You. Me. Getting to know each other better. Spending time together. Dating. Not just having sex."

He sounded so bossy and arrogant, like he was telling me instead of inquiring about my opinion on the matter, but I knew the truth. Robbie *was* asking me, and he needed to hear me say it out loud.

I swallowed hard and counted to three before reaching out to touch him. My fingertips grazed the muscles in his back before gripping on to his waist for dear life. "I want that. And I definitely want more than just sex. I want it all, Robbie."

"Thank God."

His breath skirted across my cheek before his lips were on mine, devouring them the way I'd craved earlier in the park. His tongue swept across my bottom lip before moving inside my mouth like he couldn't get enough.

His hands reached underneath my ass, and before I knew what was going on, I was in the air. I tossed my arms around his neck as he walked us toward his bed, never breaking the kiss. Our mouths were fused to one another, even as our teeth crashed.

The second he laid me down on top of the bed, my stomach growled, and I couldn't stop myself from laughing. His eyes widened as he stared at the lower half of my body.

"You're hungry," he said before smacking his head. "Of course you're hungry. I didn't let you eat."

I could have lied and said that I was fine, but the truth was that I did need food at some point or else I was going to die of starvation. "I am actually. But I can wait."

A wicked grin appeared, and he moved my tight dress all the way up my thighs, a small gasp escaping from between his lips. "You're not wearing any panties."

"Didn't want the lines."

"You're lucky I didn't know that in the limo," he breathed out, and instead of asking him why, the question died on my lips the moment his tongue touched my flesh. "I wouldn't have been able to stop myself from doing this in the backseat."

My dress was shoved up to my hips as he buried his face between my thighs. There was no slow torture, no taking his time to explore every inch of me before reaching the goods. This man dived headfirst into my lady parts and started feasting like he'd done it a million times before. I writhed on top of the bed, my hips lifting, my hands fisting the sheets with the intensity. No man had ever been so skilled at this before.

If I'd thought he was going to talk to me while he did his thing, I was mistaken. There were no words coming from his mouth, and apparently, I didn't need them. He showed me how much he enjoyed what he was doing by doing it until I came. My breath was ragged, my face felt flushed, and I swore I had his head trapped between my legs. When he moved away, his eyes searched for mine and held on as he wiped his face with the back of his hand.

I wasn't sure I'd ever catch my breath again.

"Holy shit," I said, my mouth dry.

He cocked an eyebrow in my direction. "Good?"

I stopped myself from rolling my eyes at the ridiculous question. "Uh, yeah," I answered before throwing my hands above my head and closing my eyes as I tried to get my heart rate under control.

"I want to take that dress off, but I'm afraid I'll rip it," he started before adding, "So, if you like it, you'd better get it off yourself before I do it."

Sitting up on my elbows, I gave him a tight-lipped smile. "Get all that off too." I wagged a finger at his body before I pushed off the bed and went to work on slipping out of my favorite dress.

He was undressed before I was. Standing there in all of his boxer briefs glory. He was ridiculously chiseled, like someone had carved him out of stone. It was no wonder that they'd put him on the cover of the calendar. His body was a freaking work of art. But even if it hadn't looked that way, I would have still wanted him just as badly. My desire for Robbie had nothing to do with what he'd been hiding underneath his clothes.

I stood there, struggling. This damn dress was easy to get into, but not easy to get out of. Once I finally pulled the material over my head and dropped it on the floor, Robbie's green eyes followed my every move. He looked enraptured as I stood there with only a soft nude bra on, which I quickly got rid of.

"I want to be surprised, but that dress left little to the imagination, sweetheart," he said as he took a step toward me. And then another one. "You're fucking beautiful." Another step.

"Thank you. You're sexy as hell."

Last step, and one hand was in my hair while the other splayed across my back as he dipped down to kiss me.

Both hands pulled me tighter, like he couldn't get close enough.

"Lose the briefs," I insisted between kisses, and just like that, they were gone, his dick springing free and knocking me in the thigh like it wanted my attention.

"Condom," he mentioned before breaking away and walking toward his dresser to fish one out.

I didn't want to stay standing, so I moved back onto his bed and scooted toward the headboard, hoping that the position I lay in looked attractive. When he turned around, condom in hand, he wasted no time in ripping it open and rolling it down his length.

When he reached the bed, he moved on top of my body before leaning down to kiss me, the rest of him still hovering. "More than just sex," he stated in a whispered breath.

"More than just sex," I repeated and hoped that it was.

Guys sometimes said all kinds of things they didn't really mean in order to get laid. I just hoped this wasn't one of those times.

His hand was between my thighs, and he positioned himself at my entrance before starting to push in. One hard thrust, and my mouth let out a gasp at the magnitude of taking him in all at once. Robbie did nothing gradually. It was almost like the idea of taking things slow was too torturous for him to bear.

I didn't mind. My legs wrapped around him as he moved in and out of me, his eyes opening and closing. Even with the condom on, he felt amazing.

"Kiss me." I tilted my head up, and his lips claimed mine the second I gave him the opportunity.

His tongue roamed inside my mouth, exploring, playing, feasting. I could taste myself on him.

His strong arms reached for one of my legs before he moved it to the side, forcing me to straddle his body like a scissor. Taking me from that way caused me to draw in a sharp breath.

"Are you okay?"

"Yeah. You just hit a new spot."

"Does it feel good?" he asked as he continued moving inside me, hitting that angle with each thrust.

I nodded. "Don't stop."

My words turned him on. I felt him grow thicker. One hand gripped my thigh, holding it firmly in place to the side as he plunged even harder into my body. I took it all, liking the way he touched places in me that felt brand-new.

"Sweetheart," he rasped, his pace quickening, and I knew he was close. "I'm going to …" he started, and then the words died in his throat as he came undone inside of me.

I gripped his shoulders as he twitched.

When he finished, he pulled out and flopped down beside me, his chest moving up and down rapidly. I turned on my side to face him, my hand resting on his arm.

He turned his head toward me. "I bet you're really hungry now, huh?"

"Starving."

"Pizza okay?" he asked, and I almost started drooling on the spot.

"Pizza's perfect."

"You're perfect." He pressed a kiss to the tip of my nose before hopping off the bed and disappearing into the bathroom, leaving me to bask in all of my post-orgasm thoughts alone.

Something had been missing in my life because this was the first time I'd felt truly, genuinely happy. I had been content before tonight, but it wasn't anything like this. Being here with Robbie filled a void inside of me that I hadn't even known existed. I'd thought I was fine on my own, by myself, but I no longer wanted that isolation.

I should have known that he'd screw it all up.

SELF-DESTRUCT MODE ACTIVATED

ROBBIE

MY ARMS FELT heavy. Someone was lying in them, pinning them in place. There was a weight on my legs as well. Opening my eyes, I saw long strands of brown hair strewn all over my chest. April was sleeping, her face completely relaxed. She looked so peaceful, lying there against me. I could stare at her all day.

I knew that last night had been more than just a good thing—hell, it was a great thing—but in the light of day, the passion worn off, I felt absolutely terrified. I sat there, staring at the ceiling, completely freaking the fuck out. So used to being rejected by women that I was scared to see the look in April's eyes once she finally opened them and realized where she was.

What if she hauls ass out of my apartment and never looks back?

What if it's all been a mistake?

What if I'm the mistake?

All of my defenses kicked into overdrive, my brain screaming for me to protect myself. I needed to ask her to leave, so it wouldn't be her idea to go. Reject her first before she could do it to me. As asinine as the idea should have been, it seemed like the right thing to do. Just the thought of it simmering in my mind calmed down my otherwise racing heart. Nodding to myself, I moved out from under her, knowing that it would stir her awake.

Her hand reached for my back, her fingertips brushing against my flesh as I got up.

"Morning," she said, her voice groggy.

"Morning." My tone was cold, and she picked up on it right away, her eyes narrowing into slits as she watched me. "Are you mad I stayed over?"

Was I mad she'd spent the night with me? God, no. But I couldn't tell her that. Not while I was operating in self-destruct mode. She stared at me, no doubt trying to figure out what had changed between falling asleep and waking up.

"No. But I do have things I need to do, so ..." I said, hinting that it would be nice if she left, so I could do all of these made-up things.

"So, you're saying I should go without actually saying it?"

Leave it to April to call me out. She sat up, pulling the covers over her chest. I couldn't take the way she was looking at me, her eyes filled with hurt and confusion, so I turned my back to her and started getting changed, ignoring her question.

The next time I dared to look at her, she was tying her coat over her dress and holding her heels in between her fingers.

"I'll call you a car."

I reached for my phone as she held hers in the air.

"I already did."

April was letting me know she didn't need me or my help. She'd been just fine on her own for years, and she didn't need me coming in and messing it all up.

"I know what you're doing." She poked me in the chest with one finger.

"Oh yeah? What's that?" I challenged.

"Pushing me away."

She was one hundred percent right, but I refused to admit it. *Deny, deny, deny.* It was the only way for me to stay in control.

"You want that to be true, but it's not. I just want you to leave."

Her face turned to stone, my words doing the damage I'd intended them to.

"Remember that you're the one who did this. When you're all messed up later, wondering where it all went wrong, look in the mirror."

Those were the last words she said before slamming my front door closed behind her.

I'd accomplished my mission of self-destruction. April was gone, and I was the one who had made her leave before she could do it of her own accord.

So, why didn't I feel any better?

HELL.

That was what the past few hours had felt like. Pure torment.

Since April had walked out the door, I'd spent every minute pacing my apartment. I found myself staring out the window for who knew how long, waiting foolishly for her to come back, as if that would ever happen. I'd forced her to go, and now, all I wanted was for her to return.

My phone was permanently attached to my hand, my eyes constantly checking the screen for updates. If she texted or called, I didn't want to miss it. But she hadn't done either. Not that I expected her to, but there was an extremely selfish and unfair part of me that wished she would.

I was dying inside over what I'd done, and it would take very little effort for me to fix it. I knew that she would forgive me, but I still couldn't bring myself to actually do it. My fear was more powerful than all my other emotions combined.

Just like I was sure her pride wouldn't allow her to be the first to reach out. Chasing after someone who had been unkind to her didn't seem like something she would do. April wasn't desperate or needy or codependent. I respected that actually. Couldn't even be mad about it. But, God, I couldn't stop obsessing.

I needed to get the fuck out of this apartment. Where it still smelled like her. Where my sheets were still crumpled the way that she'd left them. Where the pillow was bunched up on one side from whatever the heck she'd done to it. Where the pizza boxes were still on the floor, where we'd abandoned them after devouring every last slice. Where the condom wrapper sat on top of my dresser, tormenting me.

After pulling on a pair of gray sweats, I grabbed a hoodie and laced up my Adidas. I was going for a run. The adrenaline always cleared my head and put me in a better mood. Digging through my workout bag, I pulled out my earbuds and put them in. There was nothing like jogging through the city with some kick-ass music playing while so many others did the same.

The air was mild, so the sidewalks and streets were jam-packed. It was always like this in the city after a storm or a cold spell. One taste of semi-decent weather, and everyone flocked outside to chase it.

I found myself weaving through the crowd, almost losing my footing once or twice, but quickly recovering. It wasn't until I rounded the corner and found myself in an immediate construction zone that things got a little hairy. The music blared in my ears, and I couldn't hear anyone or anything. I needed to drown out the noise. But when I lost my balance after tripping over some broken-up concrete pieces and fell toward oncoming traffic, I wished I could have heard the warnings. A strange man's horrified expression met my eyes as he lunged forward to try to reach me before I hit the pavement.

Only I didn't hit the pavement at all. I hit steel and metal. I saw April's sweet face, her gorgeous hazel eyes, and her long hair in my mind, and I was instantly filled with regret over what I'd done that morning. In less than a second, I saw a thousand pictures, felt a million emotions, and knew exactly what needed to be done.

And then my world went dark.

NOT FAMILY

APRIL

I'D JUST GOTTEN on the phone with Sheila, figuring that it would be best not to avoid her and get the scolding over with, when she got another call and put me on hold. I waited on the other line for her to come back, but when she did, her voice was shaking.

"There's been an accident."

My brain heard what she'd said, but I didn't fully comprehend what that had to do with me.

"Okay?" I said the word like a question, still not getting it.

"It's Robbie, April. He got hit by a car."

I definitely processed that.

"What? Where is he?" I swallowed around the lump in my throat as a bunch of horrible thoughts raced through my head.

How bad is it?

What if he doesn't make it?

What if he thinks I don't want him?

What if the words I said to him this morning are the last ones he ever hears?

After getting the hospital information from Sheila, I hung up without even saying bye. She'd forgive me for being so rude. It was her fault I was in this mess with Robbie to begin with. Her and her stupid ability to see when two people belonged together.

I hated that she was right.

I hoped we still had a chance to fix this.

I knew exactly where I needed to be.

I WASN'T FAMILY. That was the first thing the hospital had asked me when I arrived and all but demanded to be taken to his room.

"You're not family."

"Not his wife."

"Not his fiancée."

Sorry.

I sat in the waiting room until Captain Alvarez and Sheila showed up, worry etched on both of their faces.

"They won't let me see him." I almost burst into tears.

"Luis will fix it," Sheila purred before giving him a shove toward the front desk. "Won't you, darling?"

"Of course," he said before pressing a kiss to her temple.

I was sure he would have said whatever Sheila needed to hear to keep her happy. Unlike the man I was falling for—the biggest jerkface on the planet who not only said mean things, but got himself hit by a car too.

Captain Luis Alvarez waltzed up to the front desk, dressed in his fireman uniform, and sweet-talked the woman sitting there. I could tell he was using all of his charm by the way she reacted to him, blushing and looking down.

"How are you holding up?" Sheila asked, and I shrugged.

"Not well," I said because I wasn't doing well. I was freaking out.

"So, are you going to tell me what happened last

night?"

"What do you mean?"

She folded her hands together and cocked her head to one side. "You didn't go to any of the planned excursions. The staff was waiting for you, and you didn't show. To anything."

"Didn't the driver tell you I got sick?"

"He did. But I know that was a lie." She gave me a pointed look. "Care to tell me the truth?"

Clearing my throat, I realized that I didn't want to get into it. Who the hell cared about last night when Robbie was in the damn hospital, possibly fighting for his life?

"I don't actually. Not right now." It was the first time I'd been so harsh with my old mentor.

I held my breath and waited for her to argue. Thank God Luis walked up instead.

"How is he? What did she tell you?" I pegged him with questions, and he held up a hand.

"He broke his wrist and has some bruising on his ribs. He'll be sore and banged up for a bit, but overall, he should be fine."

"Because he's bullheaded." It was the only reason I

could think of for why a man could get hit by a freaking car and only break his wrist. His body must be as stubborn as his head.

Luis laughed. "That he is."

"Can I see him?"

He gave me a soft nod. "You can. You have to say you're his girlfriend though. I vouched for you. He's in room 301."

I leaned up and gave him a squeeze. "Thank you, thank you," I said as I stopped hugging him. "Are you guys coming up?"

"In a bit. You go first," Luis said.

I practically sprinted toward the stairwell. I figured the stairs would be faster than an old hospital elevator.

I'D SPENT HOURS in Robbie's room, sitting in a chair right next to his bed as I waited for him to come to. The nurses told me that they'd sedated him for the pain, so they weren't sure when he'd wake up. After they reassured me that he wasn't in a coma—too much *Grey's Anatomy* for me—I relaxed as much as I could.

He was visibly bruised, and there were scratches on his face and ears. Parts of him that shouldn't have been were noticeably swollen, but I had been told that was all normal as well. Robbie's body was in healing mode.

"Visiting hours will be over soon," one of the nurses told me.

I asked if I could stay. I didn't want him to wake up alone. She said that I could, and I almost cried with relief even though I knew I wouldn't have gone far. If they'd said I couldn't be in his room, I would have moved to the main waiting area. I wasn't leaving this hospital until my man opened his eyes.

Whoa.

My man?

"April …" Robbie's scratchy voice filled the air, and I gasped out loud as he looked around, confusion etched all over his face. "Where am I?"

"You're in the hospital, you big jerk." I wanted to smack his leg, but I refrained. For his sake.

"The hospital?" His eyes pulled together as his mouth closed tight before he tried to nod, but stopped quick. "Right. I was jogging." He visibly relaxed, as if all the pieces had just put themselves in place. “I hit something. Or something hit me?”

“You versus a car. The car won.”

“I sort of remember that,” he said before asking, “What are you doing here?” For once, he didn’t sound rude or annoyed.

“Someone called Captain Alvarez. Captain Alvarez called Sheila. Sheila told me.”

“And you came here?”

“Of course I came here.” As if his stupid behavior from earlier could have been enough to warrant me giving up on him that easily. “I was worried.” I wiped at my eyes with my knuckles, but it was no use. Emotion welled up out of me, and the tears fell down my cheeks.

“About me?” He looked at my hands, which were inches from his body, but not touching him.

“Yes, you idiot. I was worried about you.” I sniffed and wished I could stop crying.

“Even after I made you leave?”

This man was going to be the bane of my existence. Testing me at every turn. Forcing me to confront my growing feelings for him.

"Yes. Even after you made me leave," I said before I started feeling a little insecure. What if he didn't want me here now? What if I'd misread the entire situation and gotten my interpretation of him all wrong? "Do you want me to go?" I asked softly, holding my breath while I waited for him to answer.

He tried to move but winced with the pain and stopped. "No." His green eyes met mine. "I don't want you to go."

All the air left my lungs, and the tears fell a little harder as my emotions got the best of me.

"I'm sorry I acted like such a dick this morning," he apologized.

I didn't want to tell him that *it was okay* because that felt like giving him a pass to do it again in the future. But I also didn't want him thinking that I was angry with him because I really wasn't.

"I think I got scared," he said, saving me from having to come up with the perfect response to his apology.

"I know."

"You know?" A small smirk appeared.

"Yeah. Which was why I was giving you twenty-four hours to pull your shit together before I reached out." I stood up from the chair, my body hovering over his in some sort of power move that made me feel like I was in control. "But then you had to go and get yourself hit by a car. Who gets hit by a car?" I rolled my eyes. "As if your job isn't dangerous enough."

He reached out for my hand and held it tight. I wasn't sure if it hurt him to do that or not, but he didn't let go as he looked at me.

"I got spooked," he whispered, like he was trying to figure out exactly what his issues were when it came to us.

"You think I don't know that? You think I don't understand the way your head works?" I tapped the side of my head with a finger for emphasis.

He'd confessed things to me, told me about his recent past, and let me see his heart. I understood that he was hurting, untrusting, and that love for him was rooted in fear.

"I didn't realize that you—" he started to explain before I interrupted whatever stupid thing was about to come out of his perfectly kissable mouth. Even with the cut on the bottom, I wanted it.

"Listen to me." I spoke in the same tone that he'd

given me before, when he'd commanded my attention, and he snapped his mouth closed. "You're allowed to get scared. You're allowed to freak out. But you're not allowed to shut me out. If you need time, you tell me. I'll give it to you. But you don't run away from me and not come back. You don't get to leave me. You don't get to give up on us without a fight."

I started to get emotional again, and I could tell that he wanted to comfort me, but his body wouldn't cooperate.

He stared at me, his green eyes turning glassy as he sucked in a breath. "That was a good speech."

I let out an awkward laugh. "I meant it."

"Come here." He pulled on my hand.

"I'm right here," I said, unsure of where exactly he wanted me.

"April, kiss me."

I leaned down carefully before pressing my lips to his gently. His hand moved to the back of my neck and held me in place. When we finally broke the kiss, he ran his finger down my cheek.

"I need to ask you for one thing," he said, and I swallowed and nodded my head. "Be patient with me. I'm definitely going to mess up, but I'm going to try my best not to."

"My speech was way better," I teased, and he laughed.

"It definitely was. I have some bad habits that I need to break. But there's no one else I want to break them for. My gut instincts are to run. But with you, my gut tells me to stay." He brought my hand to his lips and kissed the top.

"I'm not going anywhere." I hoped my words reassured him and brought him some sense of peace that I knew he struggled with when it came to relationships.

"I wouldn't let you if you tried," he said instinctively, and I knew he meant it.

If I ran away from him, I sensed that Robbie would chase me to the ends of the earth, just to bring me back. And I'd do the same for him.

How had we gone from being annoyed with one another's existence to not wanting to let each other go in a handful of weeks?

I had no idea, but I was here for it. And I wouldn't have it any other way.

EPILOGUE

APRIL

SIX MONTHS LATER

I HATED ADMITTING that Sheila had known what she was doing all along, but it was obvious that she had. She'd seen something that neither Robbie nor I could see. The craziest part was how she'd put it together from knowing us each separately and only meeting Robbie twice. It wasn't like he and I had ever met before she came on the scene and played matchmaker for the matchmaker.

Ironic, I know.

Robbie had healed from his injuries fairly quickly, which didn't surprise me. I stayed over at his apartment every night until he was better, playing nurse—and dressing up like one. He'd liked that even though he hadn't always enjoyed playing the part of the patient.

My man with the soft heart, who hated being soft.

We were going strong. Our communication and comfort were on a level I often talked about with my clients, but never experienced for myself. I'd been in love before, but it had never been like this.

"Sweetheart," Robbie's voice called out as he walked into my office, roses in hand.

"Hi," I said through my surprise. At the roses and him. "What are you doing here?" I asked as I pushed away from my desk and walked into his arms.

He kissed me, his tongue instantly in my mouth, and I had to force myself to stay standing. This man made me weak.

"I just wanted to see you. Let you know I was thinking about you."

I grinned, taking the red roses from his hand. "You could have called."

"This is better."

"Hey, Robbie," Meredith crooned as she sauntered past my open door and gave me a wink.

She'd seemed to know what Sheila had—that Robbie

and I were going to end up together. Sometimes, the people in this business were annoying and a little too self-assured, even when they were right.

"Hey, Mer," he said back, but she'd already gone to her desk.

"We're still on for dinner, right?" He sounded a little nervous, and for a split second, I thought he might be breaking up with me.

He wouldn't have brought me roses if he was going to dump me later, right?

"Yep. But don't forget that I have that client meeting at five thirty, but it should only take an hour."

He kissed me again. "Okay. I'll see you at home."

"Which home?" I asked with a laugh because we were constantly at one of our places, rarely sleeping alone when we didn't have to.

"Your apartment."

"Just because you have a key, you think you can come and go whenever you please?" I teased, but his face paled noticeably.

"Uh …" he stumbled, and I laughed.

"I was just joking," I said before adding, "I love when

you're at my house."

"Okay. I gotta go." He blew out a quick breath, looking completely distracted. "I love you."

"I love you too. Thanks for the roses."

I watched him hurry out of my office without looking back, and I wondered what had just happened. He had acted weird, and my stomach started turning as I searched for a vase to put the flowers in.

"Why'd your man practically sprint out of here?" Meredith asked as I rounded the corner into the kitchen.

"I don't know. He was being weird, right?"

She shrugged. "He's not usually in such a rush. What'd you do to him?"

"Nothing," I snarled before taking my perfect roses and putting them on top of my desk.

Meredith stayed with me until my last appointment left the premises. I called down to security and double-checked that my new patron had either driven away or gotten safely into a cab. You couldn't be too careful these days, especially being a woman.

Even though I assumed the majority of my clients were harmless, you really never knew. Being alone after hours in the office was one thing, but being alone with a man after hours was something else entirely.

"I'll see you tomorrow," Meredith said as we parted ways outside the building. Our trains headed in opposite directions.

After an uneventful train ride, I followed the underground stairs up and into the brisk evening air. My building was just up ahead, but I kept my eyes focused on my surroundings, skimming across the guys handing out flyers among the throngs of New Yorkers rushing to wherever they were headed.

Once I was inside my high-rise building, I got into the waiting elevator and pressed the button for my floor, the doors closing loudly. Some days, I took the stairs for a little extra exercise, but today was not one of those days. My feet were already aching for no real reason at all.

When I stepped out of the elevator and into the hallway, the smell of food hit my senses like a slap to the face. My stomach growled. I wondered whose apartment the delicious scent was coming from. As I reached my front door, I turned the knob and stepped inside. The incredible smell was coming from my place!

Robbie stood in the kitchen, commanding the oven and the stove, all at once, two glasses of red wine already poured and waiting on the counter. He spun around when I slammed the door, a nervous grin on his face.

"Welcome home," he said, and I practically ran into his arms.

"I could smell this all the way down the hall," I said before planting a kiss on his cheek.

He pulled out a wooden spoon and blew on it before feeding the white sauce to me.

Mmm, Alfredo.

I moaned in delight as I swallowed. "So good."

"I'm glad." He swatted my ass before telling me to get out of the kitchen. "Wine's on the counter."

"I'm going to get changed." I wanted out of my business attire and into comfy but still sexy clothes.

I kicked off my heels and grabbed a pair of thick socks from my drawer. Dropping the rest of my clothes in a pile on the floor, I pulled out a pair of black yoga pants that claimed to lift my ass and a white crop top. Robbie always stopped what he was doing whenever I wore something that showed off my stomach. Claimed he couldn't help himself. It usually led to sex. Which, trust me, I was not complaining about.

By the time I walked back into the kitchen, Robbie was plating the food. He stopped, dropping the utensils the second he caught sight of me, his eyes homing in on my exposed tummy.

"April," he growled.

"Sorry," I said even though I wasn't and we both knew it.

He squeezed his eyes shut before opening them again, focusing solely on the food. Asparagus from the air fryer—one of my absolute favorite things to eat—sat next to a pile of thick noodles, covered in homemade Alfredo sauce, which was topped with fresh Parmesan, pine nuts, and basil. When he pulled the garlic bread from the oven, my jaw dropped. There were chunks of garlic covering the slice of French bread.

"Did you make that from scratch?"

He nodded. "Yep."

Before I could ask who'd taught him, I remembered that he'd learned how to cook in the firehouse. They made family-style meals every night, rotating jobs, and he'd picked up a few things over the years.

He slid a plate in front of me and one next to me at the bar, and I grabbed my glass of wine and held it in the air.

"Thank you for dinner. You're amazing."

"Thank you for not giving up on me. For not letting me walk away. And for being the best thing that's ever happened to me," he said, and I started tearing up.

"What was all that for?" I asked, my voice emotional as we clinked our glasses together and each took a sip.

"Just wanted you to know."

Putting my glass on top of the counter, I sucked in a breath. "What's going on? Are you breaking up with me?"

Robbie practically spit out his wine. "Why would you think I was breaking up with you after I said all that and made you dinner and brought you flowers today?"

"I don't know," I said, flustered. "Because you did all those things. Are you dying? Oh my God, you're dying, aren't you?"

"No," he said with a laugh. "I'm in love with you, April. I want to spend the rest of my life with you, but it's only been six months, and I like to pretend that I'm smart instead of someone who rushes into things without thinking twice."

"Okaaaay." My heart raced inside my chest.

We'd talked about getting married down the road, but we had both agreed that it was too soon.

"I wanted to ask you something."

Why is he so nervous?

"I was thinking that we should move in together," he said, his lips mashing tight as he waited for my reaction.

"Really?" My heart still raced because I was suddenly super excited.

Moving in together was a logical next step, and the idea of having him with me every time he wasn't at the firehouse made my knees weak in the best possible way.

"Yes. I want to come home to you. And wake up next to you. And share my life with you," he explained.

This man, who had been so scared of love in the past, wanted to share all of his heart with me.

"I know we practically live together anyway, but it's not the same."

He was right. It wasn't. Knowing that we each still had our own apartment to retreat to if we needed to wasn't the same as committing to sharing one space. There'd be nowhere to run. Nowhere to hide. If things got rough, we had to come home. And home would be together.

"What do you say, sweetheart? Live with me?"

The smile on my face was so big that I could barely see. "Hell yes, I want to live with you!"

I hopped up from my chair and leaped into his arms. He was kissing me before I took my next breath.

"The next time I tell you I have something to ask you, I'm going to be holding a ring when I do it," he whispered next to my ear.

This time, my knees did give out.

But his strong arms held me firmly in place, and I knew he'd never let me fall without being there to pick me up.

This was exactly the kind of love that I helped my clients find. And now, it was happening to me. I almost couldn't believe it. I finally felt like I was living up to the quote on our office wall and the one that greeted our potential clients on our website:

Life is a puzzle. And our hearts are the most complicated piece. But they're also the most important. So many of us search for our perfect match in vain and frustration, all the while knowing that meeting the right person makes everything else click into place.

This is where the magic happens. Welcome home. Let's find your missing piece!

The End

Robbie and April were pieces of work, were they not?! But, hey, who doesn't want to break down the shell of a super-hot, grumpy fireman to get to the heart inside? And April, silly girl, we all know there's more to life than just work. LOVE is the most important thing of all. (But you can still kick ass and be successful too!)

Thank you for reading.

This book is part of a collection of stories I wrote, called FUN FOR THE HOLIDAYS! I wrote them to give you quick reads that would bring you joy and leave a smile on your face. There are twelve stories in total—one for each month of the year. You've got to read them all. And you can right now! They're all available on your favorite retailer and are coming in audio throughout the year!

Other Books by J. Sterling

Bitter Rivals—an enemies-to-lovers romance

Dear Heart, I Hate You

In Dreams—a new adult college romance

Chance Encounters—a coming-of-age story

THE GAME SERIES

The Perfect Game—Book One

The Game Changer—Book Two

The Sweetest Game—Book Three

The Other Game (Dean Carter)—Book Four

THE PLAYBOY SERIAL

Avoiding the Playboy—Episode #1

Resisting the Playboy—Episode #2

Wanting the Playboy—Episode #3

THE CELEBRITY SERIES

Seeing Stars—Madison & Walker

Breaking Stars—Paige & Tatum

Losing Stars—Quinn & Ryson

THE FISHER BROTHERS SERIES

No Bad Days—a new adult, second-chance romance

Guy Hater—an emotional love story

Adios Pantalones—a single-mom romance

Happy Ending

THE BOYS OF BASEBALL

(THE NEXT GENERATION OF FULLTON STATE BASEBALL PLAYERS)

The Ninth Inning—Cole Anders

Behind the Plate—Chance Carter

Safe at First—Mac Davies

FUN FOR THE HOLIDAYS

(A COLLECTION OF STAND-ALONE NOVELS WITH HOLIDAY-BASED THEMES)

Kissing My Co-worker

Dumped for Valentine's

My Week with the Prince

Fools in Love

Spring's Second Chance

Don't Marry Him

Summer Lovin'

Flirting with Sunshine

Falling for the Boss

Tricked by My Ex

The Thanksgiving Hookup

Christmas with Saint

About the Author

Jenn Sterling is a Southern California native who loves writing stories from the heart. Every story she tells has pieces of her truth in it as well as her life experience. She has her bachelor's degree in radio/TV/film and has worked in the entertainment industry the majority of her life.

Jenn loves hearing from her readers and can be found online at:

Blog & Website:

www.j-sterling.com

Twitter:

www.twitter.com/AuthorJSterling

Facebook:

www.facebook.com/AuthorJSterling

Instagram, Pinterest, TikTok:

@ AuthorJSterling

If you enjoyed this book, please consider writing a spoiler-free review on the site from which you purchased it. And thank you so much for helping me spread the word about my books and for allowing me to continue telling the stories I love to tell. I appreciate you so much. :)

Thank you for purchasing this book.

Sign up for my newsletter to get emails about new releases, upcoming releases, and special price promotions:

Come join my private reader group on Facebook for giveaways:

PRIVATE READER GROUP

facebook.com/groups/ThePerfectGameChangerGroup

Made in the USA
Columbia, SC
16 March 2023

13835486R00095